1

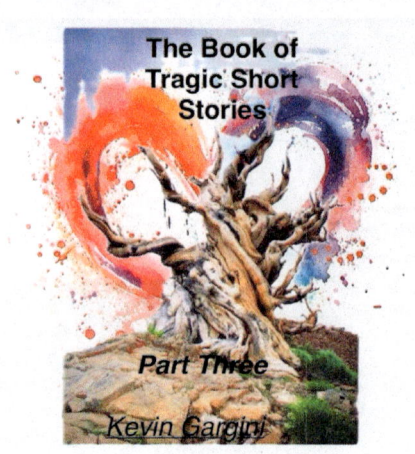

Dedication.

I dedicate this book to my lovely daughter, Poppy.
She inspires me everyday.
She makes me want to be a better person.
I love you darling.

Dad x

The Book of Tragic Short Stories
Part III

- The Graffiti Master
- The Emotion Thief
- The Best Godfather Ever
- The Accidental Boss
- Stepping Stones
- Medicine For My Pain
- In Search of Love
- Beating the Fuzz
- Zoey, My Love….
- The Pendulum of Luck

The Graffiti Master

Lethargic Leo was bored and sat in the waiting room with his angry mother at his posh school, awaiting a meeting with the top brass. He didn't want to be there, he hated school, but his mother begged him to attend the meeting. The meeting was to decide whether he gets one last chance at the prestigious school. At the tender age of fifteen he had just started his GCSEs in Year 10, but his problems had started long before.

He looked disheveled, his shirt was untucked, shoes were grubby, and his hair was a little wild. Leo didn't know who his father was, according to his mother, they had a one-night stand. Caz, Leo's mother told him that he hadn't been seen since. Deep down, Leo wanted to track him down but didn't know where to start. He always suspected his mother knew more than she was letting on. He brought it up a number of times, but she always got defensive, and they always ended up arguing. Caz had a short temper, she didn't like talking about her past, she had a bitterness which kept people away from her.

Leo had always struggled at school and was disruptive, rude and aggressive to teachers as well as students, he was like a tornado in a stately home. When he was caught with a spray can next to a freshly painted tag on the side of the science block, he knew his number was up. He was finished at the school, and he appeared to be the only one that didn't care.

The Head Teacher's Personal Assistant came into the waiting area and asked them to follow her to the meeting room. Caz and Leo walked in and sat down at the top of the table with eight people staring at them. Mr Vaughn the Head went through a list of many incidents and wanted to see remorse from the eyes of the young man sat there with his disappointed mother sat next to him, like they were on the naughty step. However, there was no remorse to be found from the adolescent.

Mr Vaughn asked Leo if he wanted to remain at the school, but Leo had no respect for anyone and he had his iPods in and wasn't listening to anyone, he hated Mr Vaughn. A true example of the distain he had for the place. His poor lonely mother just sat there speechless at her son's 'brutal two fingers up' at authority. He had blown it, but he didn't care, to him this was all a waste of time, he would happily burn the old school to the ground.

Leo may as well had stood on the desk and bared his backside at the school's hierarchy. However, that wasn't necessary as the school board turned into a firing squad and expelled the ungrateful boy. Caz didn't know where to turn and had all of those judgemental eyes staring at her. They both got up and hot stepped it out of there. At this point Leo had no chance of obtaining any qualifications and his future looked bleak.

They got into the car and Leo said to his mother,
"They were asking too many questions, it was driving me crazy, too many questions make me want to scream."

A down-beaten Caz said, "Scream all you want. Absolutely no one cares anymore. You're a stupid idiot with nothing going for you, if you weren't my son I'd have nothing to do with you."

"Bloody hell mum. That's a bit strong, chill out, it's only school."

Caz replied, "Only a school? You have no idea what I've been through to get you into that place. It might only be school now, but if you ever find work, you'll be kicked out with that dumb attitude. You're a waste of space."

"Don't worry about me mum, I'll be fine. I reckon I'll be working within a month."

Caz ended the conversation with,
"Yeah right, we'll see. Now stop boring me with your silly nonsense."

Lazy Leo spent the next week playing games online until three in the morning and then spent the day sleeping. He enjoyed it to begin with but eventually he got bored. He contacted a few of his schoolmates and met with a few in the evenings. They hung around, causing mayhem, being noisy, breaking things and then Leo got himself a spray paint. They went down to the subway and began practicing their tags. After a while Leo perfected his tag and over the next few months made sure everyone knew it throughout the local towns. He was tagging any wall, bridge and building he could.

Eventually he got caught by the police, arrested for many criminal damages and sent to the magistrate's court. As he was still under eighteen, he was given a Youth Rehabilitation Order and had to meet up with a YJS officer once a week. They educated him on the laws and how his actions affected so many people, even though he thought it was victimless. They also spoke about his lack of education and low self esteem.

The main aim was to redirect his actions into a positive and legitimate activity. Leo said he was interested in art and especially the graffiti form of street art. He liked the Banksy style and wanted to create something unique for himself. Leo got a pencil set and sketch pad and began doodling and trying new designs out. He got really into it and by all accounts he was pretty good. He was particularly good at somber and tragic scenes, or as Leo described it as "It's real."

His first opportunity came when Leo was at the youth club and the group leader gave him permission to create "a masterpiece". The leader was really supportive and told him he wanted the artwork to make them all millions, in a tongue in cheek comment.

Leo got his spray paints and some stencils he had made and went to work. He started at four in the afternoon and finished at eleven. Seven hours of hard work and dedication, it was probably the only thing he had ever done to his full ability. He stepped back with the lights looming overhead and gazed at his artwork.

He loved it, it was a picture of a couple of hoodies searching a Police Constable. The look on the officer's face was hilarious, he looked shocked and embarrassed whilst the hoodies went through his pockets. The colours were vibrant and edgy, it was fun with a little bit of menace thrown in.

The following day was Saturday and by lunchtime the youth centre was packed with teenagers laughing and taking pictures of it. They loved it and it was the talk of the estate. Even the local police officer thought it was amusing and tweeted it out on his official account.

Leo started working on other projects and when he ran out of walls being offered to him for his art, he had to go rogue. He went into Brighton which was full of opportunities. Alleyways, tunnels, old offices and discarded houses, were all available canvas' for him. He just had to keep an eye out for the police. If he received another charge for criminal damage, he would be in a lot of bother.

Some of the pictures were of people in different poses, there were paintings of love, sorrow, violence and crime. Leo was an angry young man and was filled with emotions that he didn't understand. He wanted to be loved but was afraid of being judged and discarded. He was angry and violence was exciting; he got a buzz from the adrenaline. Leo was sad and created pictures of dismay and hopelessness. He knew that happiness and sadness went hand in hand, without one you wouldn't experience the other.

Leo continued his journey of discovery in the dark world of gorilla graffiti. He had a few close encounters with the police, but he always managed to evade them. With busy Brighton having a high crime rate with drugs, violence, prostitution, burglaries and sexual assaults, it meant the police always had something more important to do rather than looking for a man with a spray can.

Around six months later there was a serious robbery down a backstreet, a knife was involved, and the victim had to go to hospital. The local reporter went to the scene and took a picture of the crime scene, in the background was a painting from Leo depicting the incident. He had even painted a likeness of the suspects. This extraordinary occurrence led to the arrest of the suspects.

A week later, a person sadly overdosed and died. In the background was a painting from Leo showing a grieving mother and father standing over the area the body was found, they were even holding a bouquet of flowers.

A month later a there was a serious fire at an old derelict warehouse, three homeless people died. On the surviving wall outside there was a picture of a group of people running in fear from a fireball. The artwork depicted the innocent victims who died a horrific death.

The list of tragedies which occurred at locations Leo had painted, and the likeness of the victims was an incredible freaky coincidence. However, can several pictures predicting the future be a coincidence?

The local press, GWS were on the path of these mysterious paintings. They had hired an art expert to travel around the city looking for more artwork from the illusive artist. Currently no body new it was Leo; he never signed his work as he didn't want the police to get wind of his exploits and arrest him.

GWS had managed to locate nine art works that they were confident was from the same artist, however, they couldn't man each picture forever because it would be expensive and take an army of people. So, they looked at the pictures and tried to guess the tragedy, which wasn't easy. They even opened it up to the public, in a spot the ball type game. It was bizarre, people were guessing on the most dark and morose events.

In the end it didn't help matters. Nobody could predict when a tragic event may happen, or even what type of incident just by looking at a picture. However, what it did do was make the unknown artist infamous. The public were all talking about the new Banksy, and Leo had to lie low for a while. He loved the fact the public enjoyed his work but was gutted he couldn't revel in the furore. He wanted to be rich and famous and show his school that he didn't need them to be successful. Whether he hated them or not, the male teachers were the only male role models he had.

Leo had produced one painting that was particularly close to his heart. It was only his fourth ever creation which was produced on a wall along the Lanes in Brighton, he produced it around three months ago. It was huge, around two metres high. It depicted a woman holding a baby in her arms. The lady was crying and looking down towards the floor, to her left. The baby's face was hidden, and the woman was dressed in a long coat with a suitcase resting on her leg. It was Leo and his mother; nobody knew about it but Leo. He argued a lot with his mum, but deep down he loved her and knew she had struggled to give him the start to life he had. He wanted to express his love for her in a type of mural.

Leo would often walk around Brighton to monitor his artwork and see if any had been damaged or painted over. When one uses the gorilla graffiti art form, they have no say as to the future of that piece, so he would survey his work. Quite often he would find other people's tags scattered around the painting like flies around a chocolate cake.

Whilst on one of his walking tours, he went to view his painting of his mother. Just as he got there, he couldn't believe his eyes as he saw Mr Vaughn walk past. He didn't want to run into him, especially after being expelled, so he ducked down like Neo from the Matrix. When Mr Vaughn had left, he spotted a hairy old man asleep. There was an empty shop with a covered doorway which was perfect for one to cocoon themselves away from the wind and the rain. Leo didn't think anything of it as it was a great place for a homeless person, however, the artwork of his mother holding him as a baby was prominent and overlooked the sleeping man. The tears were running down the face of his young mother and she was looking down at the man.

Homeless Harry had made it his patch; he had to fight off other suitors, but Harry had a reputation of being dangerously unpredictable. To be able to fall asleep in an area where people are moving around you either takes the Zen of a master Shaolin Monk or two bottles of wine. Harry wasn't a Monk so chose the latter.

Harry was an ex-serviceman and had been in the Gulf War. He didn't enjoy the desert nor the heat and when he was discharged from the army, he became a painter and decorator. He muddled away for years but after his marriage broke down, he lost everything. His devious ex-wife took the lot.

Now Homeless Harry was a hard drinking man begging and stealing his way from one day to the next. He had long greasy brown hair and an unkempt long beard. He wore dark glasses and a trilby hat, a long trench coat and had a brown holdall with his worldly belongings. He lived in the shadows and moved around when most people were at home or asleep. He would often walk past houses and glance in with envy. He once had it all and now he had nothing, absolutely nothing. The alcohol wasn't just helpful for his sleep; it also helped him forget his worries.

Normally Leo wouldn't look twice at this man or give this scene any credence, but with the freaky way some of his previous paintings had predicted the future, he asked himself the inevitable question.
"Could that homeless man sleeping peacefully under my mother, be my father?"

Leo had always wanted a successful man to breeze into his life with a zillion interesting and crazy stories and declare himself as his father. However, at this stage he just wanted anyone and thought that his gift had brought his father back to him.

Leo wasn't sure what to do, he didn't want to leave and possibly never see this man again. What if it was his father? This could have been his only chance to meet his dad, and he didn't want to lose it. Leo was incredibly nervous and the hair on the back of his neck had stood up. He didn't want to be attacked by this man, but he needed answers.

Leo gently woke up Homeless Harry, who was not best pleased. He opened his eyes and looked up, in a grumpy growl he said,
"What the hell are you doing? Leave me alone you prat."

Leo said,
"I'm sorry, but I need to talk to you. I think it's really important."

Harry shuffled around in his sleeping bag and looked at Leo. He said, "You're a bit young to work for the council. Anyway, I'm not moving, this is my patch. So, leave me alone, I just want to sleep."

Leo said, "Sir, I really need to talk to you. Let me get you breakfast. Can I buy you a coffee and a sausage roll? I'm not from the council. I just need a few minutes of your time. Come on, what have you got to lose?"

Harry replied, "If you're not going to go away, I'll have a coffee with three sugars and two large hot sausage rolls. I'm starving."

Leo made his way to Greggs and Harry sat upright; he rubbed his eyes and put his glasses and hat on. After a few minutes Leo had returned with the breakfast bounty and handed it over to Harry. Harry took the sausage rolls and devoured them with flakey pastry cascading down his black and grey beard and clinging to it like the worst decorations on a Christmas tree ever.

Leo gave him a minute and watched in horror as the breakfast was being shoved into the snarling hairy mouth. It was like feeding time at the zoo. Once Harry had completed his meal and was swigging from his hot sweet coffee, Leo said,
"Look, the reason I woke you is because I think fate might have brought you back to me. This is going to

sound really odd, so please bear with me. Sixteen years ago, you met my mother, Caz. She was twenty-one and you met her on a night out. Don't freak out, but I think you might be my father."

With that Harry started laughing and almost choked on his drink. "You've got the wrong fella mate. I'm not your father, I don't remember a girl called Caz. I'm forty-four, I haven't got any children, I think I'd know by now."

Leo found it difficult but tried to explain the bizarre occurrences around his graffiti artwork. He pointed to the painting and showed Harry his mother holding him as a baby whilst looking down on them. Harry admitted he found the painting haunting but said he didn't recognise the woman.

Leo was not taking no for an answer and was incredibly insistent. He wanted to help him; he encouraged Harry to get up and took him to the hairdressers called Barnets. The barber needed some convincing as he didn't want to touch Harry but Leo, who had made a few quid from some of his commissioned artwork, offered to pay double.

With the beard now neatly shortened and Harry's hair clipped short, he looked much better. They then went to the First Base Day Centre for the homeless. Harry was able to shower, and they gave him some fresh clean clothes. Harry looked and smelt like a new man. Whilst there Jav, a volunteer, helped Harry apply for various shelters including the Emmaus Project in Portslade.

It was Harry's lucky day. Leo was like a guardian angel. Within a few hours Harry's life had taken an upturn,

Emmaus had a room available, their philosophy was that everyone of the companions worked onsite. They had two shops, a cafeteria and a garden centre, it was an amazing place for everyone lucky enough to have the opportunity.

Harry got settled into Emmaus and Leo got him a mobile phone so they could stay in touch. Harry got a position in the kitchen in the cafeteria; he was making sandwiches and salads. Leo was so proud of Harry, his father (potentially), but Harry still wasn't convinced. Leo tricked his mother Caz to go for lunch at Emmaus and look around the secondhand shop. Caz liked rummaging through charity shops looking for a bargain, so agreed.

Caz loved the place; it was an old monastery adapted for the public to shop and eat and run by the homeless, where they also lived. Mother and son sat down in the café and ordered two portions of Welsh Rarebit and two mugs of tea. Leo was really nervous, his heart was pounding, he was reintroducing his mother and father. A shock reunion for both parties after a one-night stand together sixteen years ago. Leo didn't want them to fall in love, he wasn't expecting that at all, all he wanted was some sort of acknowledgement that they knew each other and that he had located his father. It was important to Leo to know who his father was, he needed that closure, even if it was someone who was a homeless drunk. He felt like he was missing a limb without knowing the full story.

After Caz and Leo finished off their lunch and a waitress cleared their table, Leo asked her if she could tell Harry he was there and to ask him to come over.

Caz looked at Leo and said,
"Who's Harry? Is he someone you know from school?"

"No mum, it's someone I think you know. I met him a few weeks ago in Brighton. Please don't freak out but I think I've found my father."

Caz almost fell from her seat and said, "What the heck are you talking about? Your father isn't called Harry. You've brought me here to meet someone you think is your dad, are you crazy?"

Harry was approaching the table and said hello to Leo, he sat down next to him, and they had some small talk until Leo said,
"Harry, this is my mother, Caz. Does she look familiar to you now?"

Harry looked embarrassed and realised what Leo was going on about. He said hello to Caz and looked at Leo and said,
"I'm sorry Leo I have never met your mum before."
He then wished them well and returned to the kitchen.

Caz didn't know whether to laugh or cry. She said, "You really are a plonker Leo. That is not your father. Why would you think that? Bloody hell, that was awkward."

Leo tried to explain his thinking and then started to get angry at his mother's attitude. He lost his temper and said, "Well if he's not my dad who is? Just tell me NOW!!!"

Caz said, "I couldn't tell you because it was part of the deal we had, I had to keep it quiet otherwise he would stop paying me an allowance."

"Who mum? WHO?"

Caz gave in and looked Leo in his eyes,
"I don't suppose it matters anymore, as you got kicked out of the school. But the Head, Mr Vaughn is your

father. I met him whilst working in the office when Vaughny was a maths teacher. We were both young, but he was already married, and his wife was pregnant. I had to keep it quiet, I'm sorry."

Leo looked down and with anger said,
"Oh, bloody hell, NO! You have to be kidding me.
I hate that man, why him mum? WHY HIM?"

Caz replied, "It was a long time ago, I thought I was in love, I'm sorry darling. Well, I suppose it dispels the myth about your painting becoming true."

Leo paused, he was about to agree with his mum, but then he remembered hiding behind the bin as Mr Vaughn walked past his painting on that fateful day. "Well mum, not quite……"

The End.

The Emotion Thief

Alana was born in the 80's and grew up in the countryside of West Sussex. She was an only child to parents who had left it late to have children, Rob and Rose. Their cottage was in the shadows of Chanctonbury Ring, a prehistoric hill fort along the South Downs. It would have been a wonderful place to grow up, if she had someone to play with. Without a sibling it was a lonely experience, her dog, Trent was her best friend. He was a black and white Border Collie, a friendly boy who loved an adventure.

Alana's parents were high-flyers in the insurance world and were well off. Work and wealth were their priority, Alana always felt she was a result of something they didn't really want. She was more of an accessory, like a new BMW or a Prada handbag. By the time she was in school Rob and Rose were in their fifties, they looked like grandparents at the school gate. They didn't mingle well with other parents and Alana was never allowed to have parties or sleepovers, so she struggled to form close relationships. There were girls she hung around with in school but never out of it.

Her cottage was lovely and had a big garden, it had a swing in it which Alana would spend hours on. Trent had a good life with lots of space to exercise and sniff around. He particularly loved his once a week walk up Chanctonbury Ring. It would take around fifty minutes to reach the top up the steep slippery slopes. The view from the top was outstanding and on a clear day the coast would be visible. Trent would be free to run about off the lead, he would investigate every nook and cranny, sniffing everything he could.

When Alana was in high school, she was allowed to walk up the hill by herself. She loved having the responsibility of looking after Trent and walking at her own pace. Her parents would often bore her with questions about schoolwork and exams. On her own she was free to do as she pleased. She'd often see other dog walkers and would enjoy a brief chat with some, usually about the weather or the dogs.

On paper, Alana had a wonderful life. Both parents at home, wealthy, a lovely home, achieving at school and had a beautiful dog. However, she knew there was something missing, a human companion, someone she could confide in, share secrets and dreams and just hang out with. She loved her parents although they were a little aloof, she craved a friend or sibling. The neighbours were mostly elderly and there were no children to befriend, they had grown up and moved on.

As she got older, she was ushered into a career with her parents. It started with learning the ropes, admin. A dull start to her employment career, however, she now had her own money and didn't have to pay rent at home, so she was able to save up. Living and working with her parents wasn't too bad as she was in a different department and they shared lifts, however she knew she would want her own space soon.

When Alana was nineteen, her nanna died, she was in her eighties, so it wasn't a huge surprise. Alana was upset, but not enough to cry. On the day of the funeral, her mother said to her,
"You look lovely Alana, black really is your colour. Just remember, there'll be a lot of people attending, most you won't know, so be friendly and compassionate. There are no invitations to funerals so you never know who will turn up."

Alana thought that was really odd.

"So mum, anyone can turn up. What if they didn't know her?"

Her mother replied, "Why would anyone attend a funeral for someone they didn't know? It's just family and friends who are there to say goodbye and catch-up. It's hardly a party."

Alana agreed with her mother and with father in tow they went to the funeral. It was in a crematorium where they had a small chapel. Everyone looked smart and somber. Alana barely recognised anyone, there were her family members, but also people who had known her nanna that she had never met. Everyone was polite and chatty, and as the youngest granddaughter she had a great deal of attention, she loved it. It wasn't her first funeral, but it was the only one she could remember.

Back at work there were a few young women who were nice. There were two she would meet up with at lunchtime and moan about work and boyfriends, they were called Sara and Willow. Alana was the only one who had never had a boyfriend. She'd spoken to a few boys at school, but no one had asked her out, she was labelled a *'Plain Jane.'*

Sara and Willow said she was pretty, but she wasn't making the most of her assets. They would eat their salads and sandwiches discussing hairstyles and makeup. Alana had never been too bothered before but was happy to listen to their advice. They always spoke about going on a big shopping trip to London or Bluewater to update her wardrobe, but it never happened.

There were a few single men at work, but Alana didn't have the confidence or the know how on how to flirt. She remained single and lonely. It wasn't that she didn't find some of them attractive, she was just really inexperienced.

After a few years she got promoted and had a decent pay rise with a lot more responsibilities. At the age of twenty-seven she moved into a small one-bedroom apartment. It wasn't much but a young woman needs her own space to grow and evolve. Living at home was stifling her like a canary in a cage. She wanted freedom and space to fly on her own.

Over the next few years, she went on a few dates, but nothing really materialised. She would visit her parents every weekend and sometimes took her dirty washing back for her mum to clean. Her mum liked to help, and Alana liked to be looked after. She even got herself a cat, she called it Marley. She loved Marley, he was a beautiful black cat and prowled like a panther. He kept her company and even slept in her bed.

At the age of thirty-five her mother Rose died of a heart attack. It was terrible, Alana had never felt pain like it. Her father, Rob was devastated, and she temporarily moved back into the family home to support him. Together they arranged the funeral and had made sure there was some beautiful music and poetry to read out. Alana was strong enough to stand up in front of the mourners and recite the poem, "Funeral Blues" by W.H Auden. An emotional poem which brought many to tears. As they were leaving the crematorium they'd chosen *"What a Beautiful World"*, by Louis Armstrong, it was amazing.

L
At the wake in the local pub, lots of people came and spoke to Alana. She listened to stories and relived memories with so many people, some she knew, some were strangers. With the eulogies, religious readings, and other elements of the funeral service it offered her inspiration and a renewed perspective on life. She

found the day emotional but also amazing, she loved it.

A little while later an elderly aunt died and Alana attended the funeral, she hadn't seen her aunt for years, but she wanted to make the effort. It was emotional but not for the death, Alana enjoyed the stories and the time with people in their vulnerable moments. She loved to piece together their lives, from school to work to becoming parents. It was like digging into history and seeing what these people not only brought to the world but also left. Without them, so many people wouldn't have existed, their children, grandchildren, cousins, friends and lovers. They had left a legacy. For Alana, it led to her reflecting on her own life, values, and relationships, fostering appreciation for the present.

A few years went by, and Alana was still single and now craving for more attention, the type of interactive attention she'd received from funerals. In an odd way she had missed them and wanted more. She would check on her father's health and make contact with other family members and tactfully ask about their wellbeing. She discovered that the older generation loved to talk about their health.

Alana wasn't getting the buzz she needed, she wanted more funerals to get her fix. She felt a little odd about admitting it to herself, but she had to find more. She read the obituaries in the newspapers, searched online and even drove past churches and crematoriums to see if she could attend one. It sounds desperate but she needed a fix, it was like a drug, she was addicted to the emotional distress and the sympathy.

Alana eventually found a funeral of one of her old neighbours. She'd only ever walked past her with a good morning or good afternoon, but it was enough to justify her attendance.

Alana went shopping and bought herself a new black dress, black shoes and a black hat. She was dressed for the day, but more importantly, she was ready for her fix. Whilst driving to the venue alone, she was excited and even had goosebumps. She practiced her "sad face" in the rear-view mirror and had perfected it.

Whilst at the funeral she looked around and didn't recognise anyone, Alana became nervous and thought about backing out. As she paused, an elderly lady walked past her and gave her a reassuring smile. That little touch was enough for Alana to continue into the chapel. The somber atmosphere and reflection on mortality gave her a renewed sense of purpose and appreciation for the present.

The service was lovely, and the family and friends of the deceased were visibly distressed and emotional. Alana loved to people watch and as she sat near the back she was working out who was who. There were a few young families in the front, and she thought they must be grandchildren. She had worked out a backstory when someone would inevitably ask how she knew the deceased. It was easy, she would just embellish on how close they were as neighbours.

After the funeral everyone got invited to the wake which was being held at the local sports club. The venue was a little run down, but the family had made an effort to make it look nice.
Alana had a great time, making up stories about her time with the deceased and the mourners lapped it up. She was brought a glass of wine and sat with people she had never met but was having such an intimate time with. It was incredible, she became hooked. They were sharing grief but also celebrating a life. As she left there were hugs and kisses and she felt alive.

This became a fixation, a lifestyle which continued without a hiccup for a few years. Alana would search through newspapers or online for anyone that had recently died. She now had a wardrobe full of different black outfits to choose from, and she would only attend if she could find a backstory to keep her from being found out. She didn't want to be known as the charlatan who got her jollies from attending funerals.

One day she attended a funeral in Brighton, she'd done her homework and was ready to grieve. She was doing her usual act and began speaking to a young man. At first, Alana was doing the talking but after a few minutes the man began to speak. She quickly realised she had seen him before. He'd been at a couple of funerals that Alana had previously been to.

She asked him a few questions about his story; she wanted to dig a little deeper to find out more about him. The man, called Jason, got himself a little muddled and began contradicting himself. Alana suddenly thought that this man was a fake mourner. She was annoyed that this person was taking advantage of these lovely people.

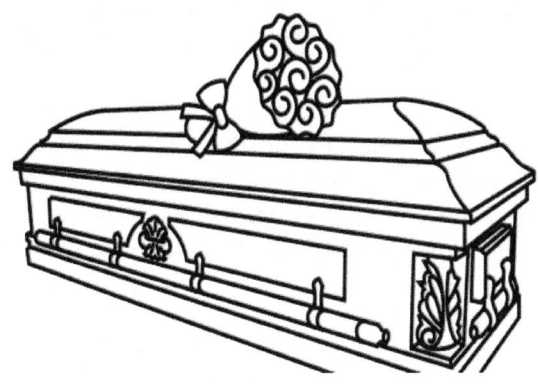

Then the penny dropped. Jason was no different to her. She had to take a few moments to understand what was happening. Alana didn't know whether to confront him or carry on with the facade. She liked Jason, he was rugged but handsome and she wanted to know why he was stealing emotions, like her.

She decided to confront him but not straight away, she thought she'd wait until they were walking to their cars.

"I know what you're up to Jason?"
"What do you mean? I'm not up to anything." Replied Jason.

Alana continued, "I know your game, you're attending funerals of people you don't know. I know Jason because I do the same. Just tell me why?"

Jason turned white and felt embarrassed, this was the first time he had ever been confronted about this. He said,
"Okay, you've got me, I know it's weird, but I just fell into it, I can't stop. Can we go for a coffee to talk?"

Alana agreed, and they drove to the pub on Devils Dyke. Whilst cradling their drinks they both looked a little embarrassed and Alana insisted that Jason explained first. He told her that his wife had died six years ago in a car crash and afterwards he was so lonely. He kept thinking about his experience at the funeral and how nice and comforting people were to him. He explained that he hadn't planned on this skullduggery, but he needed it and was searching for that feeling of compassion again.
 They spoke for hours and really had a lot in common. They swapped numbers and decided that together they could attend funerals as a couple, and they would only need one cover story between them.

Their odd relationship worked well for the next four funerals. After that they just stopped going.

They didn't need to anymore, they had found each other, plus Alana was pregnant. Their loneliness was over, the emptiness was fulfilled, their craving for love and compassion was still as strong, but the search was over.

When people ask them how they met, they say they were two lost souls that had something secret in common, their clocks stopped.

The End

The Best Godfather Ever

Igor was twenty-four years old and a bit odd. He still lived at home with his mother and worked as a librarian in a local secondary school. He had lived in Crawley his whole life, and rarely ventured outside of the town, why would he, Crawley had everything he needed. There was a bowling alley, a cinema, a leisure centre, restaurants, schools, a college, a hospital, and a few football teams. Crawley was one of the nine new towns built after World War II, it had fourteen separate neighbourhoods and was still growing, Igor lived in Tilgate.

Igor thought Tilgate was an amazing place, it had a large row of shops and had a huge park, which had a massive lake, a golf course, woods and a Smith and Western. Igor didn't have too many friends, but there was Steve and Dunc who stayed in contact with him after they had left school. No one else did, but Steve and Dunc were kind and probably felt a bit sorry for the shy reclusive singleton. Steve was a surveyor, and Dunc was a trainee sommelier in a posh restaurant in town.

Igor's father had passed away after a battle with cancer and his mother, June, was a dinner lady at the local primary school. She was an old-fashioned woman who enjoyed looking after her only child. June was always worried about Igor's future and was as happy as a pig in poo when he got a job.

Steve had been with Kim since they were in Year 10 at school. They'd fallen in love, whilst in the English class when they were forced to sit next to each other. Kim was easygoing and looked out for Igor, she found him fun but in a silly way. Their school was fairly modern, but the students didn't treat it well, there was often food and drinks thrown to the floor creating a mess, but it was dinner for the seagulls. The underpaid teachers tried their best and some of them were excellent, but many were beaten down by the aggressive attitude of some of the pupils. Igor loved it there; it was like his second home.

Igor had left school at eighteen after doing an NVQ, but he never really left, within three months he was back at the school, but this time he was on the payroll. He loved the library; he would spend hours every day reorganising the books after the ungrateful pupils had demolished his efficient work. He enjoyed the smell of the books and the silence. When it was quiet he was able to read his favourite classics. He loved Charles Dickens and Shakespeare but often enjoyed short stories written by witty, handsome, intelligent new authors from Sussex.

There was also a cute girl who worked in the photocopier room next door to the library. Her name was Sonia; she was sweet but painfully shy like a squirrel. Igor wanted to ask her out, but his self esteem was so low that he didn't have the confidence or courage to do it, however he admired her understated beauty from a distance.

Steve had big news, he told Igor and Dunc that Kim was pregnant. The boys couldn't believe it, that was proper grownup news. Igor had never had a relationship, so couldn't imagine ever being a father. Dunc had a girlfriend called Sofia, but they weren't even living together. Sofia was Bulgarian and they had met online. Steve was always the first out of the three to do things, he was the first to drive, work and move into his own house. He was more driven and ambitious than Dunc and Igor.

Time flew by and before they knew it, Kim had given birth to a beautiful daughter, and they called her Carly. Steve and Kim were over the moon, he matured overnight. Steve had an afternoon party for close family and friends to introduce Carly to everyone. However, Steve's friends were invited a few weeks later in a low-key affair. Kim was great with Carly, and they were talking about having the Christening within the next year.

Dunc asked a few questions about the Christening and then asked Steve whether it had been decided who was going to be the Godparents. Steve said they hadn't decided yet. Igor's ear's pricked up like a fox and at that point he decided he wanted to be the Godfather, but not just any Godfather, he was going to be the best god damn Godfather ever! He never thought he was ever going to be a father, so this was the next best thing.

Igor knew he had to show Steve and Kim that he would be a good choice, and he wanted to display how responsible he can be. He wracked his brain and with his impulsiveness he bought himself a cuddly kitten. Igor called the cat, Shadow. He loved that kitten, he bought all the accessories, litter tray, toys and food bowls. He took lots of pictures and made sure Steve knew how great he was.

However, it wasn't having the impact Igor wanted, Steve wasn't impressed enough, so went out to the pet shop and bought a cute chinchilla. Steve loved the kitten and the chinchilla but needed more convincing, so Igor bought a Macaw parrot. Igor's poor mother was now inundated with animals running, climbing, and flying around her house. All three were like lightning, chasing each other, fighting, and playing. Squawk, squawk, squawking, from the parrot, a crybaby of a chinchilla and a kitten that would make a squeaky noise when he was hungry. Igor was nicknamed Dr Doolittle by his mother.

Steve noticed the efforts Igor was putting in and told his patient wife, that they should consider making Igor a Godfather, Kim was not convinced. Igor upped his game; he bought Carly some lovely new designer clothes and a bag full of toys. Kim appreciated his efforts but told him not to waste his money as babies grow so quickly, and the clothes wouldn't fit Carly for long.

As the Christening got closer, Steve and Kim had to decide between Igor and Richard to be one of the Godfathers. Richard was a university friend of Steve and Igor hated him. He thought Richard looked down on him and used to call him *"The Hunchback."*

In the end, one week before the Christening, Igor was amazed when he was offered the role. They didn't think Richard cared whether he was godfather or not, so Igor's persistent had paid off. Igor was over the moon, he bought a new suit, wrote a speech and smoked a cigar. It seemed obvious that Igor wasn't completely sure what the duties of a godfather were.

The day eventually came, and Igor renounced the Devil, and he was officially Carly's godfather. He got some funny looks after the christening when he clinked a spoon onto his wine glass to announce his speech whilst at the small party. He kept it clean but relived some escapades he and Steve had at school. The audience was surprised as was Kim, who was extremely confused and gave Steve a little kick to his shin. Igor then went to the bar and bought a round of shots for everyone.

Once the big day was over, the next big event was Carly's first birthday which was a few months away. Igor had plans, he wanted to make sure Carly had a day to remember, which was unlikely as a one-year-old. If it was possible he would have bought the chocolate factory from Mr Wonka.

Kim had organised a low-key family gathering in the afternoon for Carly's birthday, but Igor begged them to pop over to his house in the morning as he had a surprise.

Kim and Steve reluctantly agreed and pulled up at 11am, just for a quick visit and a cup of tea, they knew he loved her. Igor's mother opened the door and with an embarrassed look on her face and showed them to the back garden. When they stepped out, they couldn't believe their eyes. Igor had organised through a children's farm to have an animal party. There were sheep, goats, and a donkey, it was bizarre. One-year-old Carly had no idea what was happening, but Igor's enthusiasm was infectious. Steve thanked him for his efforts but did suggest it was a little over the top.

As the years went by, the presents became more elaborate, an electric car, holiday to Centre Parcs and ringside tickets to WWE at the O2. Igor's outgoings were not huge, but neither were his wages, he soon got into dept.

By the time it was Carly's eleventh birthday, Igor drove past their house and threw a holdall full of cash onto their front lawn. He was quickly followed by a black BMW who began shooting at Igor's car. Igor span away from the scene and lost the BMW. Steve heard the commotion and peered out of his front window; all he could see was a bag on his garden. He retrieved it and the holdall was stuffed full of £20 notes. Steve took it inside and suddenly got a text message saying,
"Hi Steve, I hope you got the bag, it's a gift for Carly, love Igor."

Steve counted the money which took forever, in total there was £28,460, he couldn't believe it. He called Igor and told him to come over and explain himself. Igor said he'd pop over in the evening.

Igor waited until the coast was clear and attended Steve's house. Steve pushed Igor into the garage, and shouted,

"Where on earth has this money come from? This is ridiculous. You're a librarian in a school, how have you got £28k?"
Igor was stunned and had to think on his feet, he didn't want to tell him he robbed the hood like Robin, so he said,
"Take it easy Steve, I had a good win on the horses. It's nothing to worry about."
Steve replied, "Then why did you throw it onto the front garden? That's just weird."
Igor said, "Sorry about that, yes it was odd, but I was late for a dentist appointment, and I wanted you to have it before I spent any of it."
Steve was confused, he didn't hear the gun shots from the BMW, and didn't want to turn down £28k. To him, the money was going to be a great start for Carly when she became an adult. Steve looked at Igor and said,
"Igor, thank you for the money, but you've got to stop with all these gifts. We really appreciate it but it's too much.
I'm putting a ban on you giving Carly any more presents. From now on you must stop. Of course you can see Carly, but enough is enough."

Igor shook his hand and drove back home. Later on, that month, Richard, whom Igor disliked, called him out of the blue and said,
"Hi Igor, I hope you're well. I have good news, I'm now a dad and in a few months, we are having a Christening. Will you be the godfather?"
Igor replied, "Wow, that's a surprise. Thanks Richard. I promise I'll be a great godfather. No more elaborate presents and no more holdall's full of money. I've realised it was a little over the top."

Richard responded, "Well, that's sort of the reason. It's more of a financial decision."
Igor apologised and had to turn the offer down. He explained that he went too far and became obsessed with being the best godfather. If he had another

godchild, he'd be concerned about getting himself into trouble, he had escaped one extraordinary situation and didn't want to go back into that world again.

Around two months later, Igor had finished work and went home. As he opened the door, he realised something was wrong. He walked into the kitchen and saw two masked men standing over his mother who was tied to a chair. One of the masked men said, "we know you took our money, we need it back or your mother and you will die".

Igor replied, "It's gone, all the money has gone. I'm sorry but I can't give you it back because I don't have it."
"Tell us what you did with the money Igor? We're not playing around here, give us the bloody money!"
Igor said, "No, I can't, it's gone. I did it because I wanted to be the best godfather ever."
With that, a masked man took June into the downstairs bathroom and fired a shot from his handgun, he then walked towards Igor with the gun pointed at him. Igor had tears running down his face. He knew he was a dead man; there was no escaping his fate. When you rob a drug dealer, there's always going to be repercussions.

The masked man with a gravelly voice said,
"Was it worth it? Was it worth the end of your life?"

Igor looked over to his mantelpiece where he displayed a handmade thank you card from Carly, it said, "The Greatest Godfather Ever" on the front with a picture of himself and Carly.

Igor then responded to the gangster,
"I was the best god damn godfather ever. So yes, it was totally worth it. Screw you."

BANG!!!

The End.

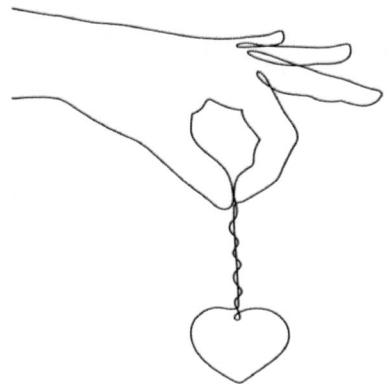

The Accidental Boss

"Grab him, get him in the van, come on... hurry up, shut the bloody door."
They held the man down in the back of a VW Campervan and Phil said,
"Stick the bag on his stupid head, hurry up, right let's go. DRIVE."

Phil was the brains of the outfit. Their job today was to kidnap a rival boss. The boss in question was the head of a British Italian crime family, The Zucchini's. However, the person they kidnapped was not the head of The Zucchini's, it was a bloke called Barry who was on his way to work.

Phil and his team were guns for hire, called the Gulls, they were a team of criminals who would rob cash vans and steal ATMs. They would use JCB's to pull the cash machines from the walls they were installed in and drive them to a lock-up. Once there they would open the ATM with a machine that looked like a huge hydraulic tin opener to access the money. Fortunately for them, they were better at theft than they were at kidnapping.

Poor Barry was a simple man, he lived with his wife and his son, Doug. He had a job and his only vice in life was going to the pub after a tough shift, he was often heard saying, "the factory is my hobby, staying sober long enough to do it, is my job."

If he was a colour, he would be beige. Barry wasn't particularly adventurous or ambitious anymore and in the oddest of ways, this was one of the most exciting things that had ever happened to him. He'd been to prison as a teenager, but his wife, son and colleagues knew nothing about it. He was just walking along a quiet road with his Pot Noodle in his pocket, minding his own business when a VW van pulled up and two men forced him into the side door. It was professionally conducted; quick, quiet and they were in and out of the area before anyone had noticed. Had it not been the wrong man they may have won a trophy at the next Gangster Awards, hosted by Danny Dyer (of course).

The van was uncomfortable and was tossing Barry around like a pair of shoes in a washing machine. The Gulls, comprised of four men with Phil their leader, he directed their every move. The driver was told to drop the parcel (Barry) off at an unused factory, where there would be someone from the rival family who would pay the Gulls for their work and take charge of the parcel.

The rival family was known as the Van Dinos. They were from Amsterdam and were huge in the drug trafficking world. They wanted to take control of the

Southeast drug supply and wanted to demolish their competitors. It was a business with high rewards for high risks. Not only did they have to protect themselves from rivals they also had the police to worry about. The courts were giving out long sentences to combat the war on drugs and firearms. Everyone involved in that world had friends who had been killed during the many conflicts, it was like kill or be killed.

Drugs was a dirty business to be involved in. They took control of communities, leaving a world of destruction. Shoplifting, burglaries, robberies, and prostitution all go through the roof as addicts will do anything for money once, they're hooked on drugs. The addiction is enough for parents to choose drugs over their children. Needles lie dangerously in parks and debts result in beatings. Area become no go zones and good honest people are frightened.

Barry was lying face down in the old smelly camper van and with the hood on his face he had no idea where he was going, he just knew he wasn't going to work. The Gulls were silent other than Phil, who was giving the driver some directions to the RV point, "turn left here, carry on over the roundabout, now turn right." The vehicles engine sounded old and was spluttering along, Barry wondered what would happen if the van broke down, would he be able to escape or would his kidnappers just kill him. A lot of things went through his mind during that short drive, he was so confused and stunned by this violation.

The camper van eventually came to a halt and Phil got out to speak to the contact from the Van Dinos. Barry got dragged out of the camper van and handed over, the money was handed to the Gulls.

Phil told Barry,

"Come on, move along. Now stand here and don't even think about running."
Phil got back into the van and the Gulls departed. Their job was completed with perfect timing and no police presence; their only issue was that they had kidnapped the wrong person. Mr Zucchini had no idea how close he came to being taken. If he had been, it may have started a turf war that would have ended many lives. Revenge is a word the Italians kill and die by.

The Van Dinos got out of their van to view their new delivery. As they approached the hooded man, they commented on how short he looked.
"He's not the size I was expecting, I always thought Mr Zucchini was over six foot." said Dick.

Benny replied, "I've seen some pictures of him, he looked huge."
Dick lent over and pulled the hood off of Barry's head. At this point, Barry was shaking, he was crapping himself. He suddenly realised that if they thought he was the crime boss, he would be probably get shot. Then he realised that when they find out he's the wrong man, they would kill him as he's a witness. Sweat was pouring off his forehead as the two men looked confusingly at Barry.

"Who the hell is this? Are you Mr Zucchini?"

Barry had to think fast, he said, "Who the hell am I! Who the hell are you? Do you know who I am? Right now, my crew will be looking for me. When they find me, you lot are screwed."
Barry had taken a chance, he thought he was facing certain death, so thought he'd go out with a bang, and go on the attack.

The two Van Dinos family members were a little stunned by the nerve of this little man. They began asking questions, but Barry wouldn't answer. They decided to take him into the house on the factory site and lock him in one of the bedrooms. They had a photo of Mr Zucchini and this was definitely not him. They wanted to talk to the big boss before making any final decision. As Barry was walked through the house, he could see it was rundown, and no one had lived there for a while. He smelt damp and there were a few pictures on the walls of the seaside and another of a family. Benny and Dick didn't have permission just to kill anyone and before they killed Barry, they wanted to get the all-clear from their boss. Bureaucracy is in every industry, even a criminal enterprise one.

The men pushed him into the room, which had a bed and a wardrobe, but nothing else and told Barry to sit down and stay quiet, they locked the door. Barry could hear the men walking downstairs as the floorboards were creaking. Barry took a moment to look around and then got up to look out of the window. His bedroom overlooked the side passage, which was a concrete path and a wooden fence separating it from the factory area. He wondered whether he could jump but the fall would likely leave him with a sprain or a broken ankle. He turned around and opened up the wardrobe, it had a few old shirts and some coat hangers, unfortunately nothing helpful.

Barry could hear muffled tones from downstairs; it sounded like two people trying to have a conversation under water. He couldn't hear what what being said but knew it was about whether he was going to live or die. A funny thing happens to a person when they are faced with death. You can either wait to die, or you can make a break for it. Do something completely out of character and give survival once last go. Barry wasn't an athletic guy, but he wasn't a dead guy either. He was still alive and had nothing to lose.

Barry weighed up whether he could overpower the two men, or whether he could survive a drop down to a concrete path. He went to the window and as quietly as he could he opened the window. It was one of the old-fashioned types that pulled up, however this one was old and was very difficult to open. He took his time and inched it open. He then went over to the bed, and he had one of those life saving ideas. He slid the mattress off the bed and threw it out of the window onto the path. He then climbed out of the window and hung on to the window ledge and then dropped onto the mattress.

He landed and fell to his left, he checked himself quickly and he was fine, no breaks or sprains. Barry got up and ran, he didn't know where he was going but ran until he got somewhere he could hide. His heart was racing and as he left the factory compound, he continued down a hill and rested in a farmer's barn. It was the first time Barry had run for years, and it was adrenaline alone that kept him going. By the time he was in the barn, he was breathing hard and was almost sick. The sweat was dripping from his head, and he had to calm down before he could check to see if he was being followed.

Eventually Barry composed himself, and couldn't believe what had happened to him, he was on his way to work in his boring job, working for his dull wife and his loner of a son. The kidnappers had taken his mobile phone so he couldn't call for help. He was all alone and checked outside but there was no one looking for him. Barry made a little area in the corner cosy and hidden so he could rest and decide his next move.

After all of that excitement, Barry fell asleep, until the beautiful bird song in the morning woke him. It must have been around five in the morning, and he decided to leave and get back home. The sun was rising over the hill like a wake-up call. He suddenly thought to himself, "I've got another chance, my family and colleagues have no idea where I am, or whether I'm dead or alive. I could start again."

With that idea in his mind, he had an extra bounce in his step. He followed the country lane until he got to a junction with a main road. He decided to stick his thumb out and see if he could get a lift hitchhiking. After around twenty minutes a lorry pulled up and said he was heading to Folkestone, as he was picking up a load in France. Barry jumped in and told the driver that Folkestone was fine.

Off they went towards Kent. There wasn't a great deal of conversation but Barry enjoyed the quiet time so he could think. He'd only been to Folkestone once before and didn't really know what was there. He didn't have any money and certainly didn't have his passport. As they got closer the lorry driver told Barry that he was pulling over at the services to grab a drink and some food and he wouldn't be taking him any further. Once they pulled up, they both got out and used the toilets and then Barry went back into the lorry park on his own. He hovered around looking for an opportunity, he was either going to jump into the back of a lorry or into the cab and hide in the sleeping compartment.

Barry had made up his mind, he was given this opportunity to start over, and he was going to do it. He also didn't want to go home and risk the criminals finding him again and killing him to make sure he never spoke about them. He was also trying to keep his family safe, but that wasn't his primary motivation. Barry had a shady history which his wife knew nothing about. When Barry, who was known as Bazza the Gear was nineteen he got two years in prison for being a getaway driver for some burglars. When he left school, he didn't have any qualifications and a few of the lads down the pub began to get in a bit of bother. To begin with they would shoplift and then they upped their game to commercial burglaries. Some of the older lads in the pub gave them some tips for places they could rob. Bazza was always mad about cars and driving, so was asked to help the boys out. After several successful raids they were eventually got caught after they became overconfident. Barry and the lads got two years in HMP High Down.

When Barry was finally released, he left his hometown for a new start in Surrey. He did the right thing and knuckled down in a factory job where he worked on an assembly line. After a year he met his eventual wife, and had truly settled down, he then became a father, and his past life was a distant memory. He was deeply in love with his wife but over time they grew apart, however he did still love her. His son, Jason was a disappointment. He was a loner who never excelled at anything, Barry was just pleased he found a job. They never fell out, they just never really talked.

Barry used his wit to sneak into a cab, the driver was busy talking to another driver, so Barry lay down in the back in the man's sleeping bag. It stunk but he had no choice, he just had to lay low until the were through the Channel Tunnel and he was in France. There was the odd moment Barry needed to sneeze, but fortunately he was able to resist. Once through to the next stop Barry got out to make his own way in France.

Barry didn't speak the lingo but fortunately he found some work on a vineyard picking the grapes from the Chardonnay, he was able to stay there to make a little money and lay low. He bought a Citroen 2CV and travelled around France, Belgium, Netherlands, Spain and Portugal. Barry became a master of reintroducing himself and lived a life of freedom. The freedom was something he never thought he'd ever get back, he loved it. He completely reinvented himself, he had relationships, met new friends and took up sports like tennis and boules. He ate a Mediterranean diet and felt as fit as a twenty-year-old. He worked as a waiter, a barman, and on numerous occasions he worked on farms and vineyards. It was a world apart from the dreary life he once had, and all because he was kidnapped by a criminal gang that mistook him for a mafia boss. Life is funny sometimes!

Several years later, Barry was given an opportunity to go to the United States. He met a lovely older woman in Portugal; she was on a European tour after her husband died. The widow, Jean, invited Barry to join her in Nevada, and he jumped at the chance. He got on really well with Jean and had never been to the States before so thought, why not.

Jean had a lovely home, her husband had been an oil baron and had left Jean with more than a few quid, life was comfortable, but Barry just couldn't fall in love with her. By now Barry was sixty-five, retirement age, but he didn't want to do nothing. Whilst spending some time in Las Vegas with Jean he became incredibly familiar with the slot machines, so much so, he found himself with a little addiction problem. He kept it from Jean but had some nasty people chasing after him. This time he had earned the attention from the local mobsters, so before he had his fingers chopped off, he took the first job he could find, he was employed as an Elvis impersonator in a chapel at Planet Hollywood. It wasn't too taxing, and he quite enjoyed joining two people in the happiest days of their lives.

Barry had changed his name so many times when travelling around Europe, and Jean knew him as Alan. Alan seemed a solid name, easy to remember and it suited him. He would marry around ten people a day, as it was Las Vegas the ceremonies only lasted around fifteen minutes. One day, a couple in their early forties came through the chapel door, it caused Barry to take a double take. He thought to himself,

"I know that man, oh my god, that's my, is it? Bloody hell, that's my SON!"

It had been over twenty-five years since he last set eyes on him, and his son, Doug must have thought that his dad was dead. Barry didn't let on and composed himself, he did his job and married Doug and his beautiful bride. Barry was close to saying something but resisted. Barry was finally proud of his son, he looked happy, handsome and confident, it dawned on him that he's missed so many years watching his son grow into this man.

Doug didn't recognise the Elvis lookalike; he had absolutely no idea his own father was marrying them. Barry usually signed the marriage certificate with his adopted name, Alan Jones. However, this time just before he put pen to paper, he paused. He then signed it, Barry Burrows. He had left a breadcrumb and hopefully awaited to see if his son would notice.

Unfortunately, Barry wasn't recognised nor was his signature, so continued his work for the rest of the day. At 6pm he completed his final wedding of the day; he went to his changing room and saw an envelope waiting on his bag. He thought it might be another demand for money, or maybe he was getting sacked, but no, it was an invite to a local restaurant at 8pm. It didn't say who it was from, the mystery deepened, and Barry put on a nice shirt and his leather coat. He thought it might be his last night on the planet due to his debts, so took his rings and watch off so it wouldn't be nabbed by a greedy coroner.

He pulled up outside of the restaurant, it was called Mon Ami Gabi, a lovely French restaurant. He was nervous, sweating a little, and his stomach was fluttering like a moth caught in a lamp shade. He looked though the window but didn't recognise anyone, but it looked busy. He walked in and spoke to the maitre d,' the suave looking gentleman pointed him towards the corner of the restaurant. As he got closer, he could see a couple, the light was dimmed, but then he realised who it was, it was Doug and his beautiful wife, Tasha.

As Barry approached, his son stood up, Barry stopped, and they looked at each other. Doug had tears running down his face, he said,
"Dad? Is that really you? You're supposed to be dead."
Barry replied, "Hello son, it is me, I have a lot to tell you. I'm so sorry I didn't get in touch, maybe you'll understand when I explain."

Doug took a step forward and held his arms out, Barry stepped forward and the two men hugged. A tear or two fell from Barry's eyes and ran down his face. He held on to his son and didn't want to let go. Tasha became emotional and began to cry whilst watching the strangest of reunions.
"Dad, please sit down, do you want a glass of wine?"
"Yes, please son, I think I need one. What wine have you got?
Tasha interjected, "it's a Sauvignon Blanc, the table next to us ordered it, so we thought we'd copy."
They sat and spoke for hours that night. It was the best wedding gift Doug could have received; he told his father about how he met Tasha; they laughed all evening. Barry opened up about his peculiar disappearance, and Doug could see why he decided on path he chose. Sometimes life offers a crossroads and during both their lives, Doug and Barry had decisions to make which takes more guts than just carrying on.

It would be a night they would never forget. Doug asked his father,
"Why don't you come home to the UK? It would be so nice to have you back in my life."

Barry paused and looked in deep thought, but he had already made his mind up.
He looked at his son and his new daughter in law and with a tear in his eye, he said, "Of course I will."

The End.

Stepping Stones

Enzo fell in love instantly. She was so beautiful; she danced around with her dress flowing behind her like a dance partner. Her hands were raised above her head, and she was laughing with her friends. The DJ played the usual wedding tunes, classics in order to get guests on the dance floor. Plenty of ABBA, Pulp, The Killers, Madness and Bananarama. It was great fun; the drink was flowing, and the dance floor was heaving.

Tanya and Teddy's wedding was a success. A brilliant day and a memorable night. Enzo wasn't much of a dancer so watched from the sideline as memories were made. Nights like this rarely come around, especially when there's such a stunning young lady catching Enzo's eye. Enzo couldn't stop watching her, she looked perfect.

Enzo was single after ending a relationship six months ago. They had been together for a few years, but it just fizzled out, like it does sometimes. Some people stick at it, others don't. Enzo wasn't in any rush to start a new relationship; he was working hard on his new business and wanted to succeed. Enzo and Teddy had known each other since school and had recently started up a wood burning stove company called, Classic Wood Burning Stoves. They had both saved hard for ten years whilst working in boring office jobs to get their business up and running. They were offering the whole shabang, sales, installation and servicing.

Teddy had been with Tania for years and the wedding was fantastic; Enzo was honoured to be the best man. They had met at college and had been inseparable ever since. Tania had a large family compared to Teddy's, and had plans for a whole bunch of children, but currently she was thriving in her career as a photographer. With the speeches completed everyone could relax and enjoy the party. Everyone was dressed up and looked fabulous, photos were being snapped at every table, the booze was flowing. The beautiful dancing princess was dancing to New York, New York by Frank Sinatra, every move she made was scintillating, however, there was a problem.

There was a man with her, he was trying to join in but was on the outside looking in, she wasn't paying him much attention. Enzo knew she had a boyfriend and should've backed off, but he didn't. He knew she liked him as she kept looking over at him and smiling and playing with her hair. Deviously he followed her when she went to the toilet, it was the only chance he was going to get to speak to her alone and he knew he would regret it if he didn't take his opportunity.

Enzo nervously approached and said, "Hi, how are you? You look like you're having a great time?"

The dancing princess replied,

"I'm great, this is great, I'm having a wonderful time. I liked your speech, you're funny you are, funny funny funny".

"Thanks, I think, what's your name?" Asked Enzo.

"I'm Libby. Nice to make your acquaintance kind sir, and what is your name?

"I'm Enzo, have you had a few champagnes?"

A tipsy Libby replied, "I may have had one or two glasses, oh wait, I might be lying. It could be three or four. Don't tell anyone."

A less drunk Enzo laughed and said, "Your secret is safe with me Libby. I will protect your dignity with my life, no one will ever know."

"That is extremely kind sir, you are as honourable as you are cute. Did I say that out loud?" Asked Libby.

"No, you didn't, don't worry. Can I have your number?"

Libby passed over her number and said, "I expect you to call tomorrow at 7pm, now I need to go for a little tinkle."

The Shakespearean exchange had ended, and with that Enzo went to see his friends. He didn't mention his exchange with the young woman, because he didn't know who the other guy was. He might have been their friend or a close relative on Tanya's side.

The following day Enzo woke up a little worse for wear, but it was Sunday so was able to sleep in and relax. He thought of Libby and remembered her beautiful smile and lovely long light brown hair; she was like a movie star. He wanted to call her straight away but thought better of it. Libby probably needed a quiet day, so he planned to call at 7pm. Enzo was really nervous; he lay in bed wondering how serious her relationship was and if she was going to remember him. She'd been quite drunk so there's a chance she's not going to have a clue who he is. Enzo considered sending a message and then tried to think about what he would say, "Hi, remember me, Enzo. Is it still okay to call you later?"

Or "As soon as I saw you, I fell in love. I can't wait to see you again."

Instead, he decided to make a cup of tea and watch the football.

Enzo couldn't talk to Teddy about Libby as she was currently the girlfriend of one of Tania's cousins; it would put Teddy into a difficult position, plus they were due to go on their honeymoon to Las Vegas the next day. Whilst watching the football, he couldn't stop thinking about Libby, nothing he did could distract him, so he sent a message, the first draft, not the overwhelmingly zealous one. Now it was a waiting game, he felt more tense than if he was in a game of Russian roulette.

For the first hour, Enzo waited patiently, but nothing. The second hour, nothing. The time was 5pm, only two hours to go until the official time for the phone call. He's now thinking about cancelling his planned call at 7pm if she doesn't reply. Maybe her phone is out of battery, maybe she's sleeping, maybe she just doesn't remember, the situation was doing his head in.

The football match was over, and Enzo was watching Roy Keane analysing the terrible tactics, he was having a rant as usual. Then suddenly his mobile phone beeped, he nervously reached for this plastic contraption that could decide his future love life. 'Message Waiting'. Enzo stood up and said out loud, "Bloody hell, bloody hell, I hope it's her, just open it. Come on."

Enzo pressed the button to open the message, his heart rate began racing, a couple of beads of sweat dripped down his forehead. The message popped up,

"Hi Enzo, I was just thinking about you. Of course you can call me. X."

Enzo smiled, he was so relieved, but that moment quickly became fear and anxiety. The pressure was now on; he had to make the call and be as charming as ever. He went to the fridge and poured himself a glass of white wine. It went down nicely, and the Dutch courage began to kick in.

At 7pm he made the phone call, Libby's memory was a little fuzzy, but she remembered Enzo. The conversation went well, and they agreed upon a date and place to meet for a drink, she didn't mention her boyfriend and Enzo deliberately didn't ask. He felt odd about going on a date with a woman who was seeing someone, but he really felt a connection. He wanted to see if there could be a long-term relationship in the making, after all she was looking at him whilst the other man was there.

The day of the date came, and they were meeting up on a Thursday night, they were going to a pub slightly out of town. Libby said it was because it was quiet and they could talk, Enzo thought it might be because she didn't want to be seen by anyone. Enzo was nervous and arrived a little early, he waited at the bar for Libby. She arrived ten minutes later and looked amazing, she wore a black dress, and her hair had been curled. Enzo didn't know whether to shake her hand or kiss her on the cheek. Libby didn't stand on ceremony and took charge, she greeted him like an old friend, a hug and a kiss on the cheek. It put Enzo at ease.

They spoke for ages about their lives and jobs, and Libby was an executive assistant with ambitions to go as far as she could. Enzo spoke about his small business and then told her about his plans for expansion when after the first location was a success. Libby was extremely impressed with Enzo's vision and future plans.

Enzo then breached the subject of Libby's boyfriend, he said,

"At the wedding were you with someone?"

Libby replied, "Yes, sort of. Alex and I have been seeing each other for a while but it's nothing serious, you don't have anything to worry about."

With that 'green light', Libby and Enzo started dating and things began to get serious. They fell in love and enjoyed spending as much time together as possible. They would go on walks down on the coast, eat beautiful meals, attend concerts and sleep in on weekends.

Enzo had his own apartment and eventually invited Libby to move in with him. She agreed and on moving day, an excited Enzo rented a van to go and help Libby with her boxes and bags. Everything was going great until he pulled up outside of her apartment building.

Libby was stood by the front door with her belongings, but then Enzo noticed a man stood next to her giving her a hard time. At first, he couldn't figure who it might be but as he got out of the van, Libby tried to shepherd the man away and back into the building. Enzo approached to find out what the problem was, as he got closer the man started having a go at him and squaring up to him, Enzo was confused but wanted to protect his girlfriend. It was when Libby said, "Alex, please just go back in and leave us alone. It's over. I told you yesterday, it's over. Get over it."

With that heartless statement, Alex looked at Enzo and said some words that stuck with him,

"Good luck mate, I was a stepping stone and so will you be."

They packed up and got in the van, during the drive back Enzo demanded to know what was going on. Libby told him that she had been staying with Alex temporarily and because of his temper she didn't tell him about moving out until the previous day. He believed her because he wanted to believe her, he loved her, but deep down he knew she had been lying to him.

Libby had settled in well and they were really happy together, Enzo and Teddy were planning to open their second store, and the money was improving every month. Libby was great and was trying to climb the ladder at work. They spoke about having children and moving into a house together. Life was good, they went on a few holidays and had a great circle of friends.

After a year, whenever they went out, he noticed that Libby was a bit distracted and looking over his shoulder at other people. At first it didn't bother him but then he remembered the wedding where they met. She was with Alex and whilst dancing she was looking and smiling at Enzo, he didn't want to believe that she would do such a thing, but she had previous for it. One day when they were in bed, he confronted Libby about it, and she said he was imagining it and that nothing was going on. Enzo wanted to believe everything was fine so just accepted it because he loved her.

Libby was an extremely pretty woman who would catch the eye of most men. Enzo wasn't surprised that she received a lot of attention, but it was the vacant looks she gave him, the silence and the lack of interest in anything he did. After a further six months things hadn't improved, and she said she was leaving him. He was desperate to know why, and she told him that she had started seeing a man at work. It turns out that Libby was always looking for the next best thing, until she got exactly what she wanted. The new person at work was a manager who had promised her promotion and extravagant holidays. He had bought her diamond earrings and Jimmy Choo shoes. He found a way to win her attention but not her love.

Enzo was incredibly upset, and Alex was proven to be right, he was just another stepping stone. In a way relieved that he hadn't got in deeper with her and got married or had children. It turned out that Libby left and carried on her climb to the top, stepping over anyone that may help her on the way. She was a popular woman with a string of admirers. Enzo's friends were supportive but unsympathetic as they were unhappy with how they had met and how Alex was treated. They cared for him but told him that "what goes around comes around."

Enzo put his efforts into the business which was thriving and in the next few years he and Teddy had set up eight new stores. They were going nationwide; it was a brilliant success. They had stores and staff in Manchester, Brighton, Exeter, and several around London. Enzo had met Sarah, a wonderful woman who he met whilst at work. She had bought her first home and wanted a log burner installed. Sarah and Enzo hit it off and they eventually settled down together. They were great together and even enjoyed watching football together. Sarah was a primary school teacher, and she loved her job. After a year together they bought a cottage and got engaged. She was slender, petite and had beautiful long brown hair, in the summer it would go light blonde. She was a gentle person who loved to read and listen to music, Sarah was a great match for Enzo.

A few years later Enzo ran into Libby whilst he was shopping for Sarah's birthday present. Libby was pushing a buggy and looked tired and dishevelled, she had gained weight, and her hair looked limp with grey streaks coming through. As they got closer Libby tried to avoid eye contact, but Enzo stopped and said,

"Hi Libby, is that you? How are you? It's been years since we last saw each other. Is this beautiful little girl yours?"

Libby glanced up and looked embarrassed, "Hi Enzo, nice to see you. I'm okay, this is Elsi, my daughter. She's two years old."

"Oh wow, congratulations, she's lovely. You're a mother, that's fantastic. How are you and the father coping with parenthood?"

Libby frowned and said, "Erm, well that didn't really work out, it's complicated, I'm single now and live on the Longmead Estate, we have a small flat above a chip shop."

Enzo smiled and said, "That sounds nice, how's work? You were a high-flyer. Are you managing director yet?"

"No, unfortunately not, I had to leave the job as the father worked there, and things got pretty messy after I met someone else, before I realised, I was pregnant. As soon, as my new boyfriend found out I was pregnant with someone else's child, he didn't want anything to do with me. But it's fine, it's just the two of us and we're getting on with it," said Libby.

"People will only see the decisions you made, not the choices you had. Take care Libby." Enzo smiled and walked off. He regretted the last sentence he said for about five minutes, but as he got into his car, he laughed to himself and thought, "what goes around comes around."

Later that evening, he was having a glass of wine with Susie and told her about his chance meeting with his ex. Susie was a little more sympathetic but agreed that you can only step on people for a short period to get what you want. She said, "external beauty has a time limit. Being a beautiful person is timeless and will follow you forever. There is nothing wrong with ambition but sometimes you have to stop chasing money. Sometimes less can often be more."

Enzo agreed with her sentiment and being a male compared Libby's life to a game of Snakes and Ladders, it's extremely difficult not to step on a snake from time to time. Enzo and Sarah went on to have three children. Libby eventually got married to a man she used to go to school with. His name was Ed, and he had a crush on Libby for years, but until she had to, she was never interested in him.

Separation causes an acceleration into desperation.

The End.

Medicine for my Pain

Tasha was rushed to hospital in an ambulance. She had a vicious stomach pain and couldn't stand up straight. The ambulance staff were panicking and had to rush her on blues and twos to the hospital. They pulled up at the ambulance entrance and wheeled her into A&E. They handed over some paperwork and put Tasha in a hospital bed and rushed out to their next job.

The A&E was heaving, babies were crying, couples were arguing, and the hospital staff were busy running around trying to help people. The atmosphere was tense, the noise was overwhelming, and Tasha felt nauseous. The pain was throbbing in her stomach, and she felt so tired, she just needed the pain to go away so she could fall asleep. There was a disgusting taste of sick in her mouth. She was taken into a room in a hurry and the professionals went to work on her. They shoved a tube down her throat and pumped out the contents of her stomach. It was horrible, machines were beeping, the doctors had face masks on, and she felt like an alien being probed by scientists at Area 51. Tasha wished she hadn't made that call, one of those clichés, "I'm going to do it", calls. If she hadn't, she might be in peace by now, the pain would have left her, and she would no longer exist. She didn't believe in heaven and thought that death would be like the final sleep.

The next few days were a blur. The nurses were throwing all kinds of medication down her throat, she was on a drip, and she was on a ward with five other people. Tasha would drift off to sleep for a few hours, until a nurse would wake her up to take her blood pressure and pulse at three in the morning.
"Leave me alone, I just want to sleep, please......" Tasha would snap in a drowsy and almost hallucinogenic state.

"Take a couple of pills Tasha, go on take a couple more, you'll be feeling worse when the side effects will show."

Was she imagining the nurses? What was real? Was she dead? Her dreams would be up there with the worst horror stories ever. Half the time she wasn't sure what was real or a dream. She kept dreaming of him. The reason she was there. Why did he leave? He'd put up with her behaviour before, he'd looked after her before, she couldn't figure out why he'd just stopped. He stopped everything, cooking, cleaning, gardening but most importantly, he stopped caring. He'd stopped loving her and she felt empty, completely lost like a handkerchief in a tornado, being spun around uncontrollably, without any hope of finding the strength to control the situation.
Tasha thought back to some of their rows, and her accusations about him of being controlling. How dare he make decisions for her, if she wanted to waste thousands of pounds then she would. How dare he

cook every meal, how dare he try and look after her, she was an adult and perfectly able to look after herself. Her friends and family always agreed with her, and actively encouraged her to kick Hugh out, they wouldn't suggest something like that unless they thought it was best for her, would they? Her friends and family knew her best after all. They didn't live with her and see 'behind the scenes' but they they definitely thought she'd be better alone.

The doctors would pop along every morning for their rounds, they hardly paid her any attention, it was, "How are you today?"

Whilst an eager to please junior doctor would look incredibly important tapping away at the keyboard. Tasha was seriously losing patience with the process. There wasn't a lot to say about the ward. It was light blue with various machines and screens adorning the large room. Sometimes some of the beds would have the curtains pulled shut, but most of the time everyone was on show. Tasha had a dark sense of humour and would joke with herself about who would die first. She even had her death list in a top five chart, from first to die to last.

As for the other patients on her ward, they were mostly elderly, they had a lot of visitors and would snore through the machines beeping throughout the night. It felt like god's waiting room; the smell felt like the devil's waiting room. Tasha desperately wanted to leave.

There was one lady on the next bed called June. She was in her seventies; she was horrible and complained about everything. The staff for reasons they soon regretted gave her a bell. If she was uncomfortable or needed anything, she was told to give a little ring of the bell, and they would come and see her. June was probably ringing that bell five times an hour with outrageous demands. She once asked a nurse to hold a tissue whilst she blew her nose. The only saving grace was that she slept a lot, at least fourteen hours a day. Those poor nurses.

Tasha was in her forties, she was single, after a recent separation with Hugh. They had been together since their early twenties, but like a lot of relationships do, it fizzled out. Hugh had moved out and moved on, he was with Julia now. Tasha had regrets about the breakup but it's over now. There's nothing she can do about it, she's alone. He was the only man who had ever loved her. Tasha only realised how much he had done until he stopped doing it. She thought about getting out on the dating scene, but her confidence and low self esteem held her back. When you start dating in your forties you are usually expected to take on a lot of baggage.

Tasha was an Estate Agent, most of her salary was based on sales. Whilst being in hospital she was only receiving her basic pay which was paltry. She had a car loan, and a maxed-out credit card bill she needed to pay. Her stress was just piling up on her shoulders, she felt like she was drowning under the pressure. Her boss had sent a card and a bunch of flowers; she'd of preferred the money.

The card said, "Hi Tasha, get well soon, we're all thinking about you. Looking forward to seeing you back in the office, don't worry about your workload, we have someone covering it.
From Dave and the team."
Due to her paranoid state, she read into it that she was no longer needed at work. It wasn't exactly a heart felt message of support, more likely a rushed response to having a card thrust under his nose.

The orderlies would take Tasha to various scans and X-rays to see if she had any other issues with her kidneys or liver. She was never updated, but she was told that no news is good news. Days turned into weeks and Tasha was suffering. She was bored, the days were long, and the food was bloody awful. She had nothing to look forward to. Her family visited her to begin with, similar to when Hugh left, but that eventually stopped and instead she received the odd phone call. Tasha would make excuses for them and say they were busy with their own lives, but their advice was like chucking a hand grenade into a room and locking the door from the outside. They weren't really there to support the downfall, it was an out of sight, out of mind scenario.

The longer Tasha was in hospital, stuck in a bed, under medication and sleep deprived, the more she felt dreadful. It felt as though her leg muscles were fading away day after day. It hurt getting out of bed, it was agonising walking to the bathroom and then adjusting herself in bed was painful, it felt as though someone was sticking a pin in a voodoo doll.

Her tiredness felt like torture, everything the hospital did made her feel worse, not better. Tasha was a prisoner in Stalag NHS. She thought about making a break for it, climbing out of the window onto the fire escape and legging it to freedom. Then she remembered that she had nothing to run towards. No partner, no pets, no close friends. A tiny depressive flat all to herself. She had grandiose plans to redecorate her home with new wallpaper, curtains and expensive furniture, but she never got round to it. It was all too much hard work. Tasha didn't like to get stuck in herself; she would rather direct others to do the sweaty heavy work.

A nurse told Tasha that a psychiatrist was in the ward to see her. They wanted to check on her progress and see how she was. She reluctantly agreed and found herself in an office with a middle-aged man. He seemed serious but friendly. They were sat in a white sterile room with two chairs and a bed. He started the conversation with the usual pleasantries and asked her how she was. Tasha told him that she wanted to leave the hospital and go home, she wanted her own bed. She was desperate for her warm duvet. Even though there wasn't much there she still preferred it to the hospital.

The psychiatrist told Tasha that they could only let her leave when they were certain that she would be okay. The discussion became a little heated and Tasha lost her temper, she shouted, "what is wrong, why won't you let me leave? I'm not sick, you're the virus!"

The psychiatrist told Tasha, "We can't just let you go. You were found close to death on your kitchen floor, you were unconscious lying in a pool of sick. You drank a lot of bleach. You tried to kill yourself."
Tasha had worked hard to blank this event out of her head. To hear it from a stranger brought back the trauma and pain she'd felt. The psychiatrist gave her a minute to let it sink in. Tasha began to cry; she knew that her situation hadn't improved, and it was likely she would try something else to make the pain go away. It again crossed her mind about her call for help, she couldn't work out if she was happy, she made it, or she regretted it.

The psychiatrist said to Tasha in an empathetic way, "convince me that this will never happen again?"
Tasha couldn't, she was told that before she was released a care package would have to be agreed and that she would have a community nurse. She couldn't help thinking about how this would all effect her life and her career. She had hoped her boss would understand, but she had doubts about his sincerity and whether he would support her. Tasha's colleagues were nowhere to be seen, the women were happy to

chuck advice at her and tell her about stories they've heard or experienced, but when it came to time and effort, they were nowhere to be found.

Tasha was wheeled back to her bed by the old porter, as she got closer, she could see a bunch of flowers on her bedside table but no card. The flowers were beautiful and were her favourite type, lilies. As a nurse walked past, Tasha asked her who brought the flowers. The nurse said she didn't know his name, but he went to get a coffee at the café downstairs. There was usually a queue there as it was a popular place.

Suddenly as she was getting comfortable in her chair, she heard a voice she recognised, it said, "Hello Tasha, how are you? I've only just heard the news; I received a message from your brother."
 She turned around and there was a man stood next to her bed holding two cups of coffee and a large slice of chocolate cake, it was her ex, Hugh, he looked worried. He said, "Tasha, I think we need to talk."

The End.

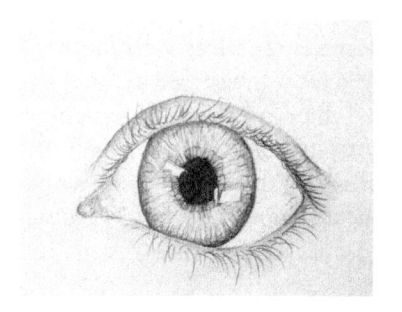

In Search of Love

The scene was a like a horror movie; three cars collided in deadly fashion. There was twisted metal, burning fuel and debris scattered across the road. Poor Zara and Jason were driving back home from a night out watching Stewart Lee at the De La Warr Theatre in Bexhill, when it happened.

Zara was driving and they were chatting away talking about the show when a car hit them head on coming the other way. It was going so fast it even smashed into the car behind them. The impact was on the driver's side and Zara was killed instantly. The car went into a spin and ended up in a ditch. Jason was knocked unconscious when his head hit the passenger side window and caused a deep wound which bled heavily.

The offending driver had been high on drugs and had drifted into the oncoming lane. The driver was killed and thrown through the windscreen as he wasn't wearing a seat belt. The car behind was in a state but the driver lived with only cuts and bruises to deal with.

The emergency services were on the scene fast. The medics did what they could at the scene and the police cordoned the road off. The fire fighters had to attend and cut people free from their congealed contraptions. They operated with the speed of lightning, attempting to save lives with their heavy-duty hydraulic equipment.

Zara and Jason were rushed to Brighton hospital in separate ambulances. Zara was declared dead shortly after they arrived, Jason was still unconscious and to help his recovery the doctors put him into an induced coma. They did this to reduce the brain's energy demands, allowing it to heal more efficiently and reduce the risk of further damage. Jason lay in a hospital, unconscious and unaware his beloved wife, Zara had died.

A few weeks later the doctors awoke Jason and when they thought he was strong enough, they broke the news about his wife. Jason was devastated; he cried uncontrollably for what seemed like days. Fortunately, he recovered well from his injuries and was allowed to go home after another week. His parents and friends rallied around him to help as much as they could.

Jason felt differently about life. He couldn't understand why this tragic event had happened to him. What had he done to deserve this, it wasn't fair. They lived a good life, they were kind to people, they were both well known in their community and now he was a widower. He'd met Zara when she was twenty, they were both students of mathematics and had met at their part time job in the Red Lion Public House at Gatwick. Whilst pulling pints and serving meals they fell in love.

Jason had always been shy and had never had a girlfriend before; it took Zara to make the first move. Whilst talking during a shift one day, they were discussing movies, and the lasted Batman was on at the cinema. It was Zara who suggested that they go together and watch it. Jason remembered being so nervous about the date, he didn't want to screw up his only opportunity.

They got married a year later and were planning to have children. When Jason had ingested the news of her death, he thought to himself, "why do I bother? We tried so hard, it's pointless". He would spend hours looking through the photo albums of their wonderful holidays and their wedding. It was so painful.

Friends and family helped him through the funeral which was an extremely difficult day. Jason bought a new black suit, with shiny black shoes and a black tie. It cost £450, he was happy to pay it for his wife but in the back of his mind he thought he'd probably never wear it again or at least he hoped.

The funeral had poetry and memories, and they held the wake at the Greyhound Pub in Crawley. There was a segregated area for the mourners and plenty of people from the past attended. School friends, college mates, colleagues, friends, and family were all present, looking smart in an incredibly sombre affair. Everyone was so kind and sweet to him, it meant a lot and in a strange way he didn't want it to end. Jason thought that if when it ends so does their marriage.

Jason had to take months off work before he could get out of his depression and fully function again. His father took him to the doctor who gave him antidepressants, and he began to exercise outside which made him feel better and he wanted to live again. The thoughts of reuniting with Zara had subsided, he burned the letters he had left for loved ones. No one ever knew how close he came to making the ultimate final decision.

Jason felt differently about life after Zara. Part of him felt like it was a new start but another part of him felt like he didn't care anymore. It gave him a strange feeling of freedom; he was as low as he could get so had nothing to lose, he felt untouchable.

He reverted back to his passion which was mathematics. He studied many different theories and became obsessed with the Fibonacci sequence. For weeks he would look into the importance of how it features in nature. The numbers and ratios in the sequence can be found in the patterns of petals of flowers, the whorls of a pinecone, and the leaves on stems. He loved finding new Fibonacci numbers in dates and structures and attempted to figure out the importance of them. It helped pass the time and gave himself some focus.

Eventually he found the strength to sort himself out and went back into work. Everyone was lovely to him, and he was eased back in. It was really nice and after a few days it was back to normal, and he was pleased for the routine it brought. However, going home was hard. Driving back knowing there was no one to spend the evenings with was a difficult way of life he had to get used to.

Four months later his grandfather died, he was ninety and was living in a care home. Jason and his family were upset but people don't tend to live forever, and his grandfather enjoyed his time on the planet. He was in the Royal Navy as a young man, he then worked on the ferries for years, he had three children and five grandchildren. His grandmother was still alive but too ill to attend the funeral, which was such a shame.

Inevitably, the funeral brought back memories of his wife's funeral, but Jason remained strong. The black suit was reused, and the service was lovely. He enjoyed meeting up with his family and this time he was able to relax and mourn his grandfather with happy memories. He loved to hear the stories about his grandfather from his old colleagues on the ferries, his Royal Navy mates had died years ago. When he got home Jason realised how much he enjoyed it, it felt strange to enjoy a funeral, but he did, it was like the old TV show "This Is Your Life."

After a few weeks he decided to accompany his mother to visit his grandmother, Jason wanted to make an effort. The care home was lovely and had a well-kept garden, there were blue hydrangeas and Japanese maple trees, with a small pond in the corner.

Unfortunately, his grandmother was unable to spend time outside as she had to stay in bed.

Jason loved seeing his grandmother, even though she wasn't well, but he enjoyed the environment. He went back several times and got familiar with staff and some of the elderly residents. He found it peaceful and calm, he spoke and listened to the residents, he even had his dinner there sometimes, it was a better option than going home.

Life inside a care home is filled with death. The longer he spent time there, the more death he saw, it lingers around the corridors. This time though the sadness was replaced with relief and happiness as they were usually suffering. Jason went to every funeral. He said it was to support the families, but the reality was he enjoyed them. Jason would stand court and relive stories about the times he had spent with the deceased. The compassion, appreciation and attention was exactly what he craved.

The more he went to, the more he sought out. He would search through obituaries for local funerals of strangers. He would don his black suit and gate crash them with made up cover stories for the real mourners.

Then things took a turn for the worse. It was a Sunday afternoon, and Jason had seen his grandmother and was walking around the garden with Ted. Ted was feeling a bit chesty, so Jason helped him back to his room. Ted lay down and Jason got him a drink of water, as he put the drink on the table Ted screamed out in pain. Jason called out for help and the onsite nurse took over. Ted wished him well and left.

When Jason got home, he was thinking about Ted, then he thought it would be nice to have another funeral to go to, he was addicted, like a user needing another hit. After all Ted was old and he'd knew him quite well, he could mingle with the family and relive old memories and good times. The following week Jason went back to the care home and poor Ted was in a bad way. Jason went into see him and Ted was breathing through an oxygen tube, he looked awful, and Jason hated to see him in pain. When Jason was alone with Ted, he knew what he had to do. He wanted to help Ted, so he squeezed the oxygen tube with his hand. Ted's face reddened and his eyes bulged, Jason squeezed Ted's nostrils with his other hand and Ted passed away with horror in his eyes. Jason tidied things up and went to see his grandmother. Around ten minutes later as Jason was leaving, he passed Ted's room and could see a few members of staff standing around Ted's bed. Jason hadn't reflected on the gravity of the situation; his brain felt like leaves in autumn.

The following week Jason had a delightful day at Ted's funeral. He met the family and spoke with great enthusiasm about his time with Ted. They laughed and cried together, drank beer and ate quiche and vol-au-vents. Jason couldn't get enough of this feeling; he was the light in the darkness for the mourners.

The following week poor old Edna became unwell and then Hilda, the list went on and on. No body suspected a thing, and when one person died another person moved in. Jason convinced himself that he wasn't doing anything wrong, he was just moving things on a bit quicker than nature would have. He just needed his grandmother to stay alive, so he had an ongoing list of victims. The system he'd created was perfect, like a conveyor belt of ego boosting satisfaction. He had nine victims under his belt over the last few years, and he was supplementing those funerals with gate crashing stranger's weddings.

It was at one of these strangers' funerals where he'd met someone. It was bizarre and towards the end of the funeral a woman confronted him.

"I know what you're up to Jason?"
"What do you mean? I'm not up to anything." Replied Jason.
She continued, "I know your game, you're attending funerals of people you don't know. I know Jason because I do the same. Just tell me why?"
Jason turned white and felt embarrassed, this was the first time he had ever been confronted about this.
He said,
"Okay, you've got me, I know it's weird, but I just fell into it, I can't stop. Can we go for a coffee to talk?"

They went for a drink at Devils Dyke to discuss their mutual strange habit of gate-crashing funerals. She seemed nice and was addicted to the attention and compassion herself. They had agreed to team up and go together for future funerals, it kind of made sense. That way they only needed one cover story.

After four funerals, which included his grandmothers, they just stopped going to anymore, they didn't need to, they had fallen in love. The need for companionship and love from strangers was no longer required, they were enough for each other. It was no longer just the two of them, Alana, his new partner was pregnant, it was perfect.

When people ask them how they met, they say they were two lost souls that had something secret in common (maybe one more than the other).

The End

Beating the Fuzz

"The sun watches what I do, but the moon knows all my secrets."
J M Wonderland.

Phil had just quit his job. He was over the moon but had a lot on his chest. He felt harshly treated but had already put his plan into action. He met up with his oldest mate Rick for a beer and a chat. Rick and Phil met in school and they both joined the Army at sixteen. It was an amazing experience, but both left at twenty-one. They were stationed overseas in Cyprus and Germany and when they were eventually back in civvies, Rick moved into cyber security and Phil joined the police. Phil jumped from relationship to relationship, but Rick settled down and had children, but the relationship ended badly. He wasn't the greatest husband and let his career take over his life, something he now massively regrets.

When the two friends got to the pub, Rick was intrigued to find out what had happened and why Phil had left the police. The men had known each other for over thirty years and had shared a lot. Rick had bent Phil's ear for a long time over his marriage breakdown and his struggles with depression. Now it was Phil's turn to rant and rave about his problems. Rick started the conversation with, "I can see you're a bit edgy Phil, what was it that annoyed you so much?"

"God, it was just the whole thing. The workload was overwhelming, but it was my colleagues that pushed me over the edge. They watched my every move. Everyday it was like Groundhog Day, the same boring people, the same conversations. They seemed content with running their lives down, it was so frustrating.

I could guess the daily conversation; I considered blowing my head off!"

"Morning, hi, morning."
"Yes, it is a lovely day, it's going to get hotter around lunchtime."
"Oh, hello. New top? It's lovely, where did you get it from?"

"Oh wow, is that the time. Right, I'd best be off. See you tomorrow.
Bye now, have a lovely evening, yes you take care also."

"Morning, it's not as warm today."
"Oh, morning, traffic was a bit heavy today."
"Hello. What have you got there? Is that something nice for your lunch."
"Morning, how was your evening?"
"Well, I didn't do a lot really, I just had dinner and watched some TV."

"Is it that time already? Doesn't it fly by. See you later."
"Yes, bye then, take care. Have a nice evening. See you tomorrow."

Phil spoke in a sarcastic tone and stressed that the rubbish continued for ever and a day. The same conversations, the same head nods, the same annoying habits. The gallons of tea and coffee.

The monotonous greetings and goodbyes. Without the job in common, none of these people would socialise with each other. Day in day out, the same faces, the same routine, it's enough to drive you potty.

Rick replied,
"What's the alternative? Ignoring one another? Grunting? High fives?"

"I don't know Rick, but I was ecstatic when I knew I was never going back to that grey, dismal, depressing, crap hole ever again." Phil said with an aggressive tone.

"Drink up Phil, it's your round. Less talking more drinking. I thought police officers loved a drink."

Phil thought out loud, "I don't even think they recognised my genius. Dumb idiots. God, I hated some of them, I really hated them. Anyway, I'm not in the police anymore, it's just me and my band."

Rick laughed and said,
"Phil, in tough times we grow the most. By the way, the barman recognises your genius, superstar, see if he can pour the cleverest man in the room two pints."

Phil replied,
"Okay, same again? When I get back, I'm going to tell you about the two most moronic ones, Hopscotch and Bailey. It was the final straw; I couldn't cope anymore."

Phil came back with two pints of beer and some dry roasted peanuts. The old, tired pub was quiet, and it still had the stale smell of tobacco from years ago. He said, "listen to this."

Phil took a huge sip of beer.

"Some people get given a label unfairly, when others earn their label."

"Hopscotch was a lanky ginger woman, she was a sycophant, trying to make friends with the decision makers. Throughout her career she told lies and gossiped to get her way. She stood in the background when situations kicked off and rarely lifted a finger to help. To say she was unpopular was an understatement. Her personal life was a disaster; she couldn't keep a friend."

Rick interrupted, "She sounds fun! Is she pretty?"

Phil laughed, took another gulp of cold beer, and continued,
"No, the criminals had dubbed her horse face, which unsurprisingly she wasn't a fan of. She was in her forties and a single mother from Crawley. The only thing going for her was her teenage daughter."

"Then there was Bailey, he was a sergeant. He pursued promotion due to the fact that he was unable to communicate with the public with any authority. Bailey was well known as the office cat, he only left the office if he had to, which wasn't very often. Bailey was also single with a couple of children; his high-flying wife had outgrown his childish ways. He was also known as the clown."

"Anyway, it was a Wednesday afternoon, and both Hopscotch and Bailey were sat in their office whilst the rest of the team were out dealing with various jobs. They were enjoying their eighteenth cup of tea of the day and suddenly there was a call on the radio from control,
"2444 Hopscotch, PC Hopscotch, over."

Hopscotch panicked as she didn't want to leave the office, but she eventually answered,
"PC Hopscotch, currently doing paperwork."
"Control continued, PC Hopscotch, please attend 12 Dorset Close. Domestic in progress. Can I show you towards?"

"Hopscotch began to shake and looked over to Bailey for an out, but he was just looking down at his computer, tapping away pretending not to notice.
Hopscotch replied, "Control, are there any other units available?"

Control said, "No one is available, I'll show you towards."

Hopscotch began to panic, "Sarge, please come with me, I can't do it on my own, it's a domestic."

Rick interrupted,
"Well, it is a domestic, two people should attend."

Phil continued,
"Bailey was stuttering and trying to think of excuses but realised he had to put his PPE kit on and attend this domestic with Hopscotch. It dawned on him that if he didn't, questions would be asked about his decision making. Horse face and the clown just wanted to finish their careers quietly and get their pensions. They had long forgotten their oath."

"From the initial call, they got to the address in a shocking twenty-five minutes.
When they knocked, a lady answered the door. Her name was Jo, and she claimed that she knew nothing about any domestic. They then knocked at the neighbours at number 11, where the original call came from."

Rick interrupted,
"Blimey Phil, is this a long story?"

"It's a lot shorter if you stop interrupting me, Rick. Anyway, there was no answer. They decided that they should leave, and they put it down to a malicious neighbour trying to cause trouble.
Whilst driving back to the office for another cup of tea, another call came out over the radio. This time it was for an 'assault in progress' at number 11 Dorset Close. Control told Hopscotch to return to the address.
When they pulled up on the road, this time it was different. The doors at number 11 and 12 were open and screaming could be heard from number 11.
They looked at each other with utter fear and short stepped it over to number 11. Bailey nervously entered the property, he kept shouting,
"Hello, hello, it's the police, what's going on?"

"As they made it to the living room they could see and hear a commotion going on in the garden. Both hesitantly went outside and tried to break up the wrestling going on between Jo and Smith from number 11. Bailey had Smith and Hopscotch had Jo. Jo overpowered Hopscotch's weak hold, broke free and walked back to her house at number 12.

Hopscotch stayed at number 11 with Smith and Bailey. Smith told them that Jo banged at his door after police drove off and as soon as he opened the front door, she attacked him, calling him a grass.

Bailey asked him if he had any injuries and Smith said Jo had pushed him several times, so Smith punched her to defend himself.

Hopscotch went back to number 12 and could see a bruise developing on Jo's left eye. Hopscotch went back to number 11, and they arrested Smith for ABH.

He was booked into custody and placed in a cell whilst other officers attended number 12 to get a statement from Jo.

Jo wasn't interested, but the two officers were persistent and talked their way in. Jo broke down in tears and became hysterical, they tried to calm her but had to call an ambulance. Whilst they were waiting, Jo began to talk about her husband and how they had a huge row. They asked where the husband was, Jo screamed and said he was in the bathroom. The two officers went up to see what was going on. The officer opened the bathroom door to find a man slumped in the bath, stabbed to death."

"Jo had killed her husband, and Hopscotch and Bailey had arrested the man who called the police. A magnificent own goal even for them. They were already a laughingstock. They ended up suspended from duty, under investigation."

Rick finished off his second pint, which ended in a large burp. He said,
"Bloody hell, I remember seeing that murder on the news, it never mentioned the cock up."

"Well, it wouldn't, the police would keep that under wraps, to save embarrassment. I just couldn't tolerate it anymore, if the public could see how lazy some of them are, they'd be uproar. That's just one of many stories; I could write a book!
I had to leave for my own sanity," replied Phil.

"I don't blame you. Another pint? Come on Phil, keep up. I fancy a proper session today."

Phil picked up his glass and downed the rest of his drink whilst Rick was at the bar. Phil looked in his bag to check the stuff he had smuggled out of the police station was still there. He wanted to tell his oldest mate but wasn't sure how he would react.

Rick returned with a couple of pints and two shots of Jägermeister. Without a word both men looked at each other, picked up their shots and downed them.

Rick said, "So tell me, how did you leave? Did you have a big row?"

Phil replied, "There was no argument, I had plenty of annual leave in the bank, so I tapped the sergeant an email, saying that I was leaving and not coming back."

Rick asked, "Was that it? It doesn't sound very dramatic. Didn't you want to make a stand?"

Phil said, "Yes, I did, but I also knew there were some items in the evidence room that could be quite useful. You can't wait for the perfect moment, you take the moment and make it perfect, Zoey Sayward said that, my ex liked her.
So anyway, I went down to the pub and had a few drinks whilst waiting for the morons from my office to go home. I then went back into the police station; there were other officers working but I just avoided them. I went into the evidence room with my hood up and took this."

Phil lifted up a brown leather holdall, which had been placed under his seat. He held it with one hand and tapped it with the other, like he'd just won a prize.

Rick smiled but looked a bit confused, he asked, "So, what is it? What on earth have you nicked?"

Phil moved the glasses to the side and put the brown leather holdall on the table. He looked down and unzipped the top. Rick looked around the pub to make sure there was no one too close and stood up, learning over the bag. With both hands he opened it up to get a good look. He stared at the contents for around five seconds and then sat down, he puffed his cheeks out and looked at Phil.

Phil zipped the bag up and placed it back under his chair. He looked over and Rick had turned white. Rick took a massive gulp of beer and said,
"Bloody hell mate, if that's real then you're looking at twenty years inside. What the hell are you going to do with it?"

Phil was calm and spoke with authority, he replied, "You and I are going to sell it. I've met some people through my job, and I've made a few connections. Tonight, we're gonna sell it and make £200k. I need your help though Rick."

"Wow, that's a lot of money Phil. How are we going to do it? Where do we need to go? What am I going to do?"

Phil replied, "I need you to act as my security. I've got a crossbow in the motor. Everything should go fine, but it's best to be prepared. The two guys are meeting us here at 10pm. They're going to have a drink at the bar and when they leave, we're going to follow them. My car is closest to the door, so you can hang back a little and grab the crossbow. I'll make the transaction."

Rick grabbed his pint and took a sip, "These guys, are they serious Phil? Will they have guns?"

"I suspect they will have Rick. But trust me, try and relax and within an hour we will be loaded. They know we're ex-squaddies, so they know we can handle ourselves."

Both men sat back in silence and even though they were drinking they were staying sober enough. They spoke about what they were going to do with their share of the money. Rick wanted to buy Crypto currency, but Phil quickly talked him out of wasting his money on that scam, he told him it's basically a Ponzi scheme.

They spoke about different cars they could buy, holidays they could go on and Phil joked about getting his teeth done in Turkey. It might have been the drink talking but Rick said,
"I've got an idea; it's been on my mind for a while. How about we go into the property conversion business? We can make one bedroom into two and two bedrooms into three."
Phil responded, "I don't know anything about the building trade, how would we do that?"

"Well Phil, we make a bedroom out of the kitchen."
A confused Phil asked "Okay, where would the kitchen go?"
A smug Rick said, "That's the beauty of this idea, people in the city eat out or get takeaways, they don't need a kitchen. Imagine it?"
An unimpressed Phil said, "No, I don't think that would work. What is wrong with you? You can't have a house without a kitchen, that's crazy, even bedsits have kitchens."
A laughing Rick replied, "Well it was just an idea, keep your knickers on."

Before they knew it, it was 10pm.
Five minutes later the pub front door was opened, two men walked in. They were medium build and looked fairly smart, they were in their thirties. Phil looked over at Rick and gave him a subtle nod. They never made eye contact with the two men, but they followed them outside around ten minutes later.

Rick went to the car as planned and quietly grabbed the crossbow and hid it behind his back. He was careful because if the strangers saw it, they might think they were being robbed. Phil walked over to the men; they had a brief chat and exchanged bags. Both parties had a quick glance at the transaction and Phil turned and walked back to his car. The other two men got in their Range Rover and left the car park, hardly a word was spoken.

Phil and Rick looked into the bag, then looked at each other and began to laugh. They had just made £200k and it all went to plan. No violence, no shootings and no police getting in the way. It was perfect. They agreed that Rick was going to hold onto the money for at least a month. He trusted Rick and knew neither of them would ever let anything get in between them. Phil thought that when the police realised that the evidence had disappeared, it wouldn't be long before his house would be raided and searched. Phil had to use his own ID pass card to gain entry to the seized property room, so quite rightly he would be suspect number one.

However, Phil was a clever lad and just before he had sent his resignation email to his sergeant, he had sent an email to HR to apologise for losing his ID card and requesting another. He knew that sending the email after 4pm would be a safe bet that it wouldn't be read until the next day. Then after he came back and entered the property room, he hid his ID card in the locker room. Whilst there he took out a few of his belongings which he needed to keep safe and away from prying eyes. If his colleagues had got to them first, he would have been in bother.

Phil had sowed doubt into the investigation and without CCTV, forensics, an admission, witnesses, money or the stolen seized items, there would be no evidence of him being involved. The only person that could give him up would be Rick, and he trusted his life with Rick.

Around a week later, as expected, Phil received an early morning knock from the police. They had obtained a warrant and searched his house from top to bottom, without success. Phil also knew that there would be surveillance watching his every move. He kept up his daily routines, Rick stayed out of the way and after a few weeks they had moved on to another suspect. Patience is key when it comes to the police, funding is tight and new crimes come in to investigate and take preference.

Around a month later Phil and Rick met up to split the money 60/40, in favour of Phil. They discussed the investigation and how they should be careful when spending the money. If Phil started to drive around in a Lamborghini, it might raise one of two eyebrows.

Whilst life carried on as normal, Phil played a few gigs with his band and Rick continued to go to work. They met up to play golf and arranged to go on holiday to Barbados for two weeks, all inclusive. They had plans to invest some of their money on a Golf Course.

Whilst out in Barbados they hired a car so they could view a couple of investment opportunities. They had smuggled some money into the country, so they were ready to make some serious commitments.

By the time they had got back to the UK, they had invested around £100k between them on a Golf Centre with driving range and gym. They had a friend on the island called Justin who was going to oversee the business.

Life was good for the two friends, more than what could be said about Hopscotch and Bailey. They were both found guilty of gross misconduct and were given the boot. It was in the newspapers and made them unemployable. Hopscotch had nothing in her life after her daughter left home, and Bailey had a sister that financially supported him.

The only problem on the horizon for the two long term best friends was a woman called Amy. Amy was a beautiful lady who breezed into Phil's life for a second time. They met years ago, but this time she was single. Whilst Phil was going for a jog around the park, he noticed a woman having a picnic with two children. He recognised her at once; his heart rate went through the roof. Suddenly and instantly, he was transported back to when they were young. Her hair was long and tied up, she looked like Natalie Portman.

Phil stopped to catch his breath and just watched quietly from a distance, whilst they laughed and ate together. He didn't want to disturb but had to speak to her; he didn't want to lose her again. Phil cautiously approached and said,
"Hi Amy, how are you? It's been such a long time, you haven't changed one bit."
Amy looked up and was shocked to see Phil, she said, "Oh my! Phil, how are you? It's been ages, I'm good thanks, these are my kids. Why don't you sit down and join us."

They spoke for ages, the children entertained themselves in the adventure playground and Amy and Phil got reacquainted. It was perfect, they just clicked, the timing was perfect, and they both knew that this was the start of something new, something that could have happened years ago.

They were talking about what they had been up to for all those years and all the funny times from their past. That moment was precious and ended with a kiss goodbye. As Amy got in her car, they looked into each other's eyes and she said, "You will call me, won't you? The last time I saw you Phil, was when you were Rick's best man at my wedding. That's crazy!"

The End.

Originally written for a 600-word short story competition.

Zoey, my love...

I first noticed her at work, she was only sixteen, I instantly fell in love. She was petit with long brown hair and had a wild edge to her. She sat on the bar (a bold move but her pretty smile made time stand still), whilst the restaurant manager, Nigel, held court.

Her name was Zoey, and she was the newest member of staff. She was our new waitress. An extremely quick learner and hard worker. Her brother worked in the kitchen. I had to break up their fighting every now and then, Zoey had a difficult upbringing and was scintillatingly feisty.

I was nineteen and studying at university. I worked at the restaurant every weekend; it gave me some money for a few student nights out during the week. I loved university but I couldn't wait to get home and see Zoey at work.

Not only was there an age difference, but there was also my girlfriend, Louise. I had been with Louise for over a year, and we loved each other but I was a terrible boyfriend. I was young and stupid; I focused on myself rather than giving her my all. Louise was my first long term girlfriend, so it was all new to me.

During the next few months, Zoey and I got closer and closer. I would pick her up and drop her off from work to save her a taxi ride. I would manipulate the rota so she got the hours she needed and so we could work together. I couldn't help myself, the excitement I had every time I saw her was like being shot out of a cannon. My heart went into overdrive, and I fell in love. She was so sexy, too sexy, it drove me insane. My immaturity couldn't compete with the social expectations.

I was her supervisor and broke the management code. I kissed her at a party. It was wrong but I didn't care. My manager told me the next day to be careful. Not long after she moved to Manchester with her best friend's family, and we lost contact. In her early twenties she made contact with me and made it clear she wanted a relationship.

Looking back, she should've known better, she knew I was in a relationship, but she didn't care. The problem never went away, I was still in love with her, but it couldn't happen; I had just got married and became a father. The torment this caused me was something no man could cope with. When my marriage broke down a few years later, I contacted her, but she had just got married and was pregnant. It just wasn't meant to be.

I longed for Zoey for years, the distance between us prevented an affair. The further apart, the more perfect she got.

Now in her late thirties, Zoey made contact and informed me she had just got divorced. I was still married to Izzy, we'd been through a lot, and we gave it another go, when we both thought all had been lost.

It was never going to happen with Zoey.

I don't know if it was love or lust, but I for years it screwed me up. It affected my marriage, my metal health, and my attitude.
I've now blocked her on Facebook. I don't fancy her anymore, maybe it was just lust. It had been a relationship that spanned over three decades, but in reality, it never got started. I will always have the thought of "What if?"

It all feels so futile. It's a shame.

Goodbye my darling Zoey.

The End

The Pendulum of Luck

Dean was knackered after work. He was in his thirties, a project manager and had just completed another eleven-hour day. He was going to head home but decided to stop off for a beer before he went back to his wife. Dean wanted to unwind and didn't want to go home in a mood and annoy Lisa. The only time they ever row is when he comes back in an irritable and impatient state. It only takes Lisa to ask him how his day was, and he explodes. Dean wanted to avoid any unnecessary drama, poor Lisa didn't deserve it. They'd been married for ten years so they knew each other's bugbears.

On his way home he often drove past a pub called The Dog and Duck. It always caught his eye as they had beautiful hanging baskets with luscious purple, fuchsia flowers, but this time he stopped. He pulled into the car park, walked in and noticed the football was on the TV. The pub was old fashioned, with a dart board and tankards hanging from the ceiling, but he liked it, it was quaint. He said,
"Evening, I'll have a pint of lager please, how's the match?"
The barman started to pull the pint, looked over to him and said,
"The games good, it's still 0-0 but it's end to end. Who do you support?"
Dean replied, "I'm a Villa fan, but I want Palace to beat United, I would love it if they got relegated."

The barman handed the pint over to Dean and said, "That would be funny, I'm a Palace fan, so I obviously want the eagles to win."
Dean paid and sat down on a bar stool, took hold of his cold beverage and gulped a quarter of it down. He felt better already.

A few minutes later another man walked in, he knew the barman's name, "Evening Mohammad, I'll have a pint of lager please?"
Mohammad replied, "No problem, how have you been Evan?"
"I'm okay, I've had a long day."
Evan sat down at the bar and spoke to the barman about the match.

The game was exciting, and Palace took the lead just before halftime. It was just the three of them and a couple in the pub who were sat near the back. They were deep in conversation and were oblivious to the football.

During halftime, the three men commented on the game, and each had their moment to explain how Palace should play in the second half. As the second half kicked off, Dean finished off his pint and was about to leave. However, he was enjoying himself and instead of going home, he thought he'd have one more pint and watch the rest of the game. As the barman handed him his lager the other customer, Evan said,
"I should really go home, but I think I'll have one more and finish the game off. I think United will make a comeback."

The couple who was sat in the corner drifted off home and the game ended with Palace winning the match 3-1. Evan and Dean said their goodbyes and left in their respective cars. Evan drove the eight miles home in his BMW without incident and after some food, he went to bed.

Dean only had six miles to travel; however, he never made it home. A woman called Johanna intercepted his journey. Her boyfriend had just broken up with her in the same week she'd lost her job. Her life was in tatters; she had been drinking and was walking down the road after buying some cigarettes. She stopped to light one and began to cry, she was in her fifties and realised that she had lost everything. Johanna began to scribble down a goodbye note to her adult daughter, however she hadn't finished it and held it in her hand. She looked down the street and saw some headlights driving towards her, she had one of those moments where she thought no one would notice if she was dead. The car was almost upon her; Johanna stepped out onto the road and was hit by the car. She smashed into the windscreen and was flung into the air where she span around and crashed headfirst onto the tarmac. Her head collapsed like an eggshell and bled out. She died almost instantly; the handwritten note blew away like a leaf in a hurricane.

Dean hit the brakes like a formula one driver and a few cars travelling in the opposite direction screeched to a halt. Dean froze and before he knew it the police and ambulance with their flashing blue lights were on the scene. The road was closed off; the ambulance had taken Johanna away and the police officer approached Dean with a breathalyser. He began to sweat; he thought that he could be in big trouble.

The officer told Dean to give a long continuous blow into the contraption, he then waited whilst his intoxicated breath was being analysed. The officer then showed Dean the outcome, it was positive, he blew 44. Just over the legal limit, however that didn't matter, he was over. The officer arrested him on suspicion of causing death by careless driving while under the influence of alcohol. His heart was pounding, and regret filled his dizzy mind.

Dean was arrested and handcuffed, he couldn't believe what was happening, what an end to what was a relaxing and pleasant evening. He was taken to Crawley custody and dumped into a cell. The cell was grey and cold with a thin uncomfortable mattress and a smelly blanket; there was nothing Dean could do other than wait. He was locked up for the first time in his life like a common criminal. He reflected on his life whilst just having four dull walls to stare at. It didn't take him long to figure out what was important to him, it was his wife, Lisa. Not his stressful job. It paid well and he had spent years working on his ability, but to what cost, we're all important until we're not there. He had plenty to talk to Lisa about, if she still wanted him.

The following morning, he had been given a duty solicitor and was advised to go 'no comment'. The solicitor, Des, had the unfortunate news to confirm that the victim had died and the charge carried a life sentence. Dean almost collapsed, he never had it confirmed that the woman had died up until that point and the thought of a lifetime in prison was overwhelming to him. He became lightheaded and his hands started to shake.

Dean was charged and released on bail to attend court for his plea hearing. Dean pleaded not guilty, due to the fact, he believed that Johanna had stepped into the road on purpose rather than his careless driving. He accepted that he blew over the legal amount, but that would just be a driving ban and a fine.

Due to Dean's not guilty plea, his hearing would be at Hove Crown Court with a twelve-person jury. Des and Dean had six months to prepare their defence and find something in Johanna's life that would point to her wanting to end her own life. It sounded a dreadful way to go around things. He knew the drink-driving was something he should be punished for, but he was adamant Johanna stepped in front of his car. Dean told his solicitor, "Why should he go to prison for her selfishness?"

The court case came around quicker than they had expected. They had spoken to her ex-boyfriend, ex colleagues and a few family members. They had a defence ready with mitigating circumstances; however, they didn't have anything concrete, nothing written in stone or even paper.

The morning of the court proceedings was awful; he had a meeting with his solicitor and met the Barrister for the first time. The jury had been sworn in, and Dean had to sit in the dock. There were a lot of people in the courtroom, and they all stood up as the judge walked in. The judge and the barrister's had their wigs on, and it looked very archaic and traditional.

The opening speeches were delivered by the prosecutor and defence barrister's, outlining what and how they were going to prove their arguments. Dean was incredibly nervous, and he felt uncomfortable in his new grey suit he had bought for the occasion. Straight away he disliked the prosecution team, they looked cocky and stated they wanted the maximum sentence for him. They wanted to make an example of him and casual drink-drivers. There was something about the prosecutor, he sounded familiar but looked strange due to his poncy wig. Then it suddenly hit him, the prosecution barrister was Evan, from that fateful night in the pub watching football. Evan who too had drunk two pints and drove home. Now it was the same Evan who was trying to put him in prison for years and completely destroy his life. It could have easily been Evan sitting in the dock instead of Dean.

As the court case went on, various witnesses were called in and gave evidence. Some were there to give a good character witness testimony to Dean and others were there to suggest that Johanna was not the type of person who would want to commit suicide.

Then there was John Rix, a witness for the defence. He was asked questions about his relationship with Johanna. He really didn't want to be there but was summoned, he recounted their last encounter.

John said it was a brief conversation at his front door a day after he had ended the relationship, and the night of her death. He claimed she had been drinking and wanted to get back together. When he told her no, she said she was going to kill herself. He said,
"Don't be like that Jo, you just need to talk to someone."
Johanna replied,
"Talk to who, who can help me?"

"Anyone Jo, just talk to anyone. It will help."

"You sound ridiculous John. Shall I talk to the milkman?"

John said he was tired and just wanted her to leave, so said,
"If you want."

Jo replied in a sarcastic tone, "Hello Mr Milkman. I'm not very happy, I'm going to kill myself.
Or,
Hello Mr Postman, I'm sad today, I'm going to kill myself.

How the hell do you think they're going to bloody help?"

John admitted he sounded flippant when he said,

"Well, I don't know, maybe the milkman will give you a free milkshake. I don't care, just leave me alone."
He paused, then said, "I regret it now, but I shut the front door and went to bed."

It wasn't until the penultimate day when Des received an email with a scanned picture of the goodbye note that Johanna had written seconds before stepping into the path of Dean's car. They had to get the original, which Des spent the night retrieving from a dog walker who found it the day after the incident. When it was exhibited at court, it was enough to win the jury over and find Dean not guilty. Johanna's death was recorded as self inflicted by the coroner, and the letter she wrote was handed to her devastated daughter.

Dean was a free man and had escaped years behind bars. Instead, he received what all first-time drink-drivers get, a fine and a short driving ban. Lisa stuck by him and she was now pregnant. He had left his job and had begun a gardening business. It was demanding work, but he was happy, and a master of his own future.

A few years later he ran into Evan once again. This time it was at a local children's playground. Dean had taken his young daughter for a walk around the park and stopped at the playground as she loved to play on the swings. After a few minutes, a young boy ran up to the empty swing and shouted loudly for his dad. The dad strolled over to help his son into the baby swing, and it was Evan.

Both men looked at each other whilst gently pushing their children and instantly recognised each other. Two men who had been through a lot together, who had never really been introduced. Evan looked sheepishly at Dean and said hello. After some awkward moments, the men spoke about the incident and the court case. Evan apologised for his robust approach in seeking a long custodial sentence but countered that he had not started his career well as a barrister, he was under a lot of pressure. He ended up reverting back to being an on-call solicitor, the work was interesting, he just had no need for his wig anymore.

Dean accepted the apology and told Evan that in a strange way the whole event made him focus on what he found important in life. They spoke about luck and how it could have been Evan sat in the dock. Neither of them ever drank and drove again and the realisation of how it can collapse everything they'd worked for like a game of Jenga, was a real wake-up call they needed. Evan spoke about the burnt toast theory, and how a negative experience can be turned into a positive.

Over the years their children became friends, and eventually so did the men, after all, they shared a joint hatred of Manchester United.

The End.

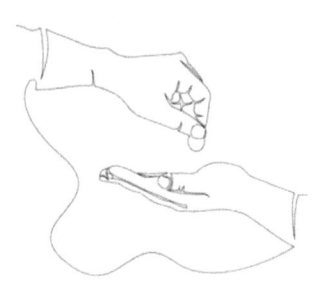

Bonus Story from Part II

The Shopping Stalker

Doug was a quiet guy who worked as a park ranger. He was in his late thirties and had managed to get through his life so far as a singleton. Unfortunately for Doug, his mother had recently died from lung cancer. It really shook him but as a woman who smoked twenty cigarettes a day for the last fifty years, it didn't come as a big surprise.

Doug had never moved out and became the man of the house at twenty-five after his father Barry, left without a trace. They all knew he wasn't enjoying life and would spend more and more time at his local boozer rather than going home. One day he was there; he went to work and just never came home, he was fifty. It was worse than a death, because they didn't know where he had gone, whether he would come back or if he was dead, it was like a ticking time bomb. They had the police looking for him with posters up everywhere with a picture of him asking "Have you seen Barry Burrows?" Unfortunately, it didn't work, nothing worked, it really hurt them.

Doug's mother had a part time job at the local Co-op and Doug took charge of the household bills. It was a lonely life, he didn't really have friends, there were some people he knew from school but everyone else had moved on. Living with his mother was easy, he had his lunch prepared for him, dinner was ready when he got home from work, and the washing and cleaning was all done, it was like he had never grown up.

They would spend the evenings watching Coronation Street and The Repair Shop, among other mundane TV shows. They never went on holiday and only went out for meals if it was one of their birthdays, they always have the rump steak. This went on for years and before he knew it his mother had passed away and he was the last person standing. He didn't even have any pets to care for. Neighbours worried about him and thought he would get depressed and end it all. Realistically, they were more worried about him leaving his gas on and blowing the whole street up.

Colleagues from work had attempted to set him up on a few dates but with his low self esteem, lack of energy and mediocre looks it never worked out. Doug just didn't seem too bothered about it. He continued to live his life and before he knew it, he was staring down the barrel of his fortieth birthday.

His hobbies included watching TV and reading car magazines. Doug wasn't interested in politics, sports, current affairs or music. He would listen to Radio 4 every now and then. When you live a life without interests, you become exactly that, uninteresting. How can you hold a conversation with someone when you have no interests? You can't!

At least Doug worked. At the age of eighteen he applied for a job via the local Job Centre. The job role consisted of keeping the local parks tidy, emptying bins, cleaning graffiti off the playground and locking the gates at sunset. Not being very ambitious, Doug just continued to work in the job and had now completed twenty years. His colleagues liked him, he was helpful and pleasant, he was just beige, very much like a glass of still water, useful, necessary but uneventful.

After Doug's mother had died, he had to make his own lunches. Everyday he would eat cheese and pickle sandwiches, an apple and a slice of cake. He hated going shopping and wouldn't know what to buy. He usually just bought ready meals like Chili-con-Carnie, chicken curry or spaghetti bolognaise for his dinners. Great meals if cooked from scratch, but the microwave versions were bland and boring. He lived a life that was worthy of a fart in the wind, he inspired nobody, he hurt nobody and would eventually leave the earth without a trace.

One evening after work he popped into the local Tesco's to buy his dinner. As he walked around with his basket, he noticed a woman with a large red coat with her hood up. He didn't usually look at other people, but this person was acting strangely.

She was following an elderly man and picking up the exact same shopping as he was buying. It didn't look like they knew each other, and the elderly man was none the wiser. Doug for once in his life was intrigued by this scenario and couldn't help but watch it unfold; it was like car-crash TV.

The man picked up butter, cheddar cheese, a half loaf of white bread, a tin of tomato soup, a tin of chicken soup, rice, potatoes, mushrooms, swede, onions and razors. The lady had the exact same items, Doug thought that this was no way a coincidence. For some reason she was copying him. He watched them go to the self-service checkouts, pay and then leave separately. Doug shook his head, and carried on buying his chicken curry, pickle and cheese. He drove home and whilst eating his dinner he couldn't stop thinking about the lady in the red coat. What a strange thing to do, he thought, and more importantly, why?

As the days continued in the same monotonous fashion for Doug, he had to go back to Tesco's. It was after work so around the same time as usual. As he was paying for his selection of ready meals, he saw the woman in the red coat enter the store. He watched her walking around with a basket in her hand. She didn't appear to look at the food items on the shelves, she was looking at people. After a few minutes, she locked eyes on a middle-aged woman and again went around the store picking up everything the lady chose, including deodorant and cat food. He was fascinated by this peculiar behaviour. However, he drove home and ate his spaghetti bolognaise.

A few weeks had gone by and whilst back at Tesco's after work Doug was a bit annoyed. The shop had shuffled the stock around as they do every now and then. He let out a sigh as he couldn't find the pickle. Just as he looked up, he noticed a red coat disappear behind the next aisle. For a brief moment he thought it might be the shopping stalker but carried on with his shopping.

When he got to the self-checkout till, he was loading his shopping into his bag for life. A red coat grabbed his attention, the woman was packing her shopping away, 3x ready meals, cheese, pickle, toilet rolls, white bread and some Mr Kipling Bakewell Slices. It was exactly the same as his purchases. He had just become the victim of the shopping stalker, he didn't know whether to laugh or cry.

As he left the store, he decided to wait for the lady in the red coat, he was going to politely confront her.

"Excuse me, hello, hello, excuse me."

The woman in the red coat looked startled, she looked at him and suddenly realised her cover was blown.

"Oh, hello. Err. Yes, what do you want?"

Doug replied, "Hello, hello".

Both had the social skills of an anxious hermit.

"I was just wondering what you were doing?"

Red coat replied, "Shopping, I've been shopping, what do you think I'm doing?"

Doug said, "I know you're shopping, I just wanted to know why you follow people around and copy their purchases".

"I don't, I don't know what you're talking about", she stuttered.

Doug replied, "I bet you have the exact items in your bag as I do in my bag."

"No, I don't, leave me alone", and with that the thirty something oddball lady got in her Ford Fiesta and drove off.

Doug wasn't used to confrontation, and this was a major incident for him in his drab life. He got in his car and drove home; he had to have a strong cup of tea to calm down. To him, that episode was like bungee jumping off the Sydney Harbour Bridge, what a rush!

The weeks continued and life went back to normal, work, Tesco's, home, dinner and bed. That incident was still on his mind, and it was the first time he held eye contact with a female for so long.

A month later he was in Tesco's, and lo and behold Red Coat was already in there. Doug noticed she was following a younger man; he was in his late twenties. He caught them up and followed her. It didn't take long for Red Coat to see him. She looked startled but did something he didn't expect.

Red Coat approached him and said, "Shush, don't say anything, I'm in the middle of something, this one's exciting."

Doug didn't say anything, he just nodded and followed her following a man in his twenties. He was thinking how odd this must've looked but it was also strangely exciting.

Was Doug turning into an adrenaline junky?

Doug didn't do the full shopping stalk; however, he did copy a few items. He picked up orange juice, Rustlers Cheeseburgers, bread rolls, Dairylea, yogurts, pizza and Doritos. It was unusual for Doug, but he was willing to jump into the deep end (he supplemented it with a few ready meals), he just wasn't ready for anarchy.

Once the shopping stool had left, Doug and the red coated lady paid and stood outside the store looking at each other. Doug started to giggle, and the surprised woman giggled back. He felt alive, it was so weird.

Doug broke the laughter and said, "Hi, I'm Doug, this is so odd, how long have you been doing this?"

Red Coat replied, "I'm Tasha, I don't know really, maybe a few years, it's just something I started to do when I was bored."

Doug said, "But don't you end up with loads of items you don't need?"

"Well Doug, that's part of the fun. I get to try food and recipes I would never normally eat, and I can usually find a use for most things. I only follow the basket carriers. If I copied the trolley pushers, I'd end up with loads of nappies and wine."

Doug asked, "have you ever been caught before Tasha?"

"Only by you Doug, it's not exactly illegal. Most people just keep their heads down and pick what they need and leave. It's good fun, my diet is so varied now, I never know what I'm going to eat for dinner."

There was a perfect pause for most normal people to swap numbers or go for a coffee, but Doug wasn't normal. He said, "Well, it was nice to meet you, see ya." With that they got in their cars and left.

When Doug got home and munched into his pizza and Doritos, he thought to himself how nice it tasted. He swigged down a glass of orange juice and made Dairylea and pickle rolls for his lunch the following day. Wow, he thought, a change actually feels quite nice. He contemplated taking on this new challenge but thought he'd sleep on it.

The next day whilst working in a park, he sat down and ate his lunch, he hadn't eaten rolls for years and he loved them. They were soft and squidgy and made him remember eating them at school. That was definitely a win for the shopping stalker. That night he had a chicken curry as he didn't want to overdo it, but he was looking forward to the Rustlers burgers for the next night.

After a few days he had to go shopping again, he usually went every three days. As he pulled up to Tesco's he picked up his bag for life and thought to himself he was going to go for it, he was going to shopping stalk. He grabbed a basket and looked around, just as he did a man in his fifties walked past him. This was the man he was going to follow.

Doug didn't want any strange interactions with a stranger, so he played it cool. He held back and subtly watched as the man picked up some potatoes, carrots and a large onion, Doug copied. The man then walked to the bakery and chose a baguette and a pack of croissants, Doug copied. Next the man walked over to the sauces and picked up a Rogan Josh curry sauce, some microwaveable plain white rice and a pack of papadums. The man then chose some toothpaste, deodorant and some hair gel. Doug watched and thought, in for a penny, in for a pound. They then completed the spree with a carton of milk and a box of Chocolate Cornetto's. Doug had done well and hadn't been noticed. He kept his distance at the checkout and walked back to his car.

He sat in the driver seat and surveyed his receipt. He thought the man must've been a vegetarian and due to his investigation skills, he was going to make a veggie curry, with rice and papadums. The only thing he wasn't sure of was the hair gel; he had never bothered too much with his hairstyle before.

However, a successful shopping stalk had been completed, he wanted to tell Tasha, but didn't have her number.

Doug loved this new way of life he had adopted, and it gave him a new lease of life. He was a risk taker; the sky's the limit. He found himself communicating with people more often and he was enjoying learning new recipes to cook. He had learnt how to cook a Chili-con-Carnie from scratch, and it fast became his favourite dish. He was trying new breads and meats he hadn't eaten for years. Only last week he ate a rack of ribs, it blew his mind, his hands and face were covered in BBQ sauce, but he didn't care.

The other day he was stuck in a traffic jam and the car next to him had the radio on, it was playing "Wish You Were Here" from Pink Floyd. As it ended, the DJ said, "That's one of Absolute Radio's favourite songs".

With that, Doug turned his radio on and found Absolute Radio. The following song was Beetlebum from Blur, then Kula Shaker, Oasis etc. He loved every track they played; a new avenue of interest had opened up for Doug.

Around six months later, Doug had brought new clothes and had begun to style his hair like Suede's brilliant singer, Brett Anderson. He looked good and for the first time in his life, females were paying attention to him. He felt confident and relaxed in his new persona.

A year later, he ran into Tasha again, she looked different. It was summertime so the red coat was back in the wardrobe. She had beige trousers on and a black vest type top on, her hair was tied up and she looked great.

Doug waved to get her attention, but she took a few seconds to realise who he was.

Tasha said, "hiya, it's Doug, isn't it? You look different, how are you?"

With that invitation, Doug told her how his life had changed after he began to shopping stalk, he thanked her for liberating him.

Tasha was a little taken aback but smiled and was pleased with his news. This time the new improved Doug wasn't going to miss his opportunity, and they exchanged phone numbers.

He eventually made contact, and they started dating. They couldn't stop themselves though and when in a restaurant would copy what the table next to them had ordered. They would laugh and exchange plates with a playfulness Doug hadn't ever experienced. They would hold hands and take pictures of each other trying new dishes like escargot and squid. They wanted to capture that moment that would never happen again. It was wonderful. They would even go to the cinema and watch whatever film the couple they were stalking chose, even down to the same snacks.

Eventually things were getting more serious, and they decided to go on holiday together, but they didn't know where. Whilst at a local travel agents they were flicking through various holiday destinations. It wasn't until a couple in their thirties had sat down and decided they wanted to go to Las Vegas. Tasha and Doug looked at each other and laughed. They waited for the couple to complete their booking and then sat down with the travel agent and said,

"We want to go to Las Vegas, in fact we want to book the exact holiday as your previous clients, down to every last detail."

The travel agent looked confused and said, "you want to book their holiday?"

"Yes, we do, absolutely everything." Said Doug.

"Are you sure? They are planning to…"

Tasha interrupted, "Don't tell us. We don't want to know. We want to experience our first holiday together as a unique and complete experience that we want to capture as the holiday progresses. It's all about the moments, you never get them back."

"As long as you're sure, I'll arrange that for you now, it will be a life changing experience for you", said the travel agent.

The holiday came around quickly and before they knew it, they were on the plane heading towards the United States. They saw the couple they holiday stalked but kept their distance. They had a beautiful hotel, with a lovely view of the swimming pool and neon lights in the distance. It was perfect, they were having a great time. After their first week there was a message for them at reception. They thought it was unusual. It said a car would pick them up the following day to take them to Planet Hollywood and they were to dress to impress.

Whilst at dinner that night they were guessing what it could be, they'd obviously booked something with their secretive holiday stalking. They couldn't wait and the next day they were dressed up and were picked up by a limousine. There was Champagne on route and when they arrived at Planet Hollywood it was decorated with an altar and white balloons in a huge arch. It suddenly dawned on them that they were just about to get married.

Doug was in shock and said, "OMG Tasha, do you want to get married, bloody hell, we've never even discussed it. What shall we do?"

Tasha was also in disbelief, but was calmer than Doug, she said,

"Doug, we met this way and it's gone pretty well ever since. We can't break the run; it will lead to bad karma. Let's do it!!"

With that Doug kissed Tasha, they held hands tightly and walked towards the aisle. Music from Elvis Presley was playing in the background and there were some people either side ready to witness their leap of faith. The service was conducted by an old man dressed up like Elvis, they found it funny but beautiful, and they were pronounced husband and wife, they kissed and knew they had made the right decision. As they walked back down the aisle, they saw another couple awaiting their turn. Both couples smiled at each other, and the other man said, "Didn't we see you at the Travel Agency a few months ago".

Doug smiled and said, "No, I don't think that happened, good luck." Tasha giggled and held his hand a bit tighter. As they walked off, they were handed their Marriage Certificate, they laughed and looked for Elvis' signature, but of course it was signed by the old man, *Barry Burrows*.

The End.

Thank you for making it to the end. I hope you have enjoyed it.

This is the third instalment of the trilogy. I hope to have many more stories in the future.

Take care.

Kevin

THE BOOK OF TRAGIC SHORT STORIES (NEW)

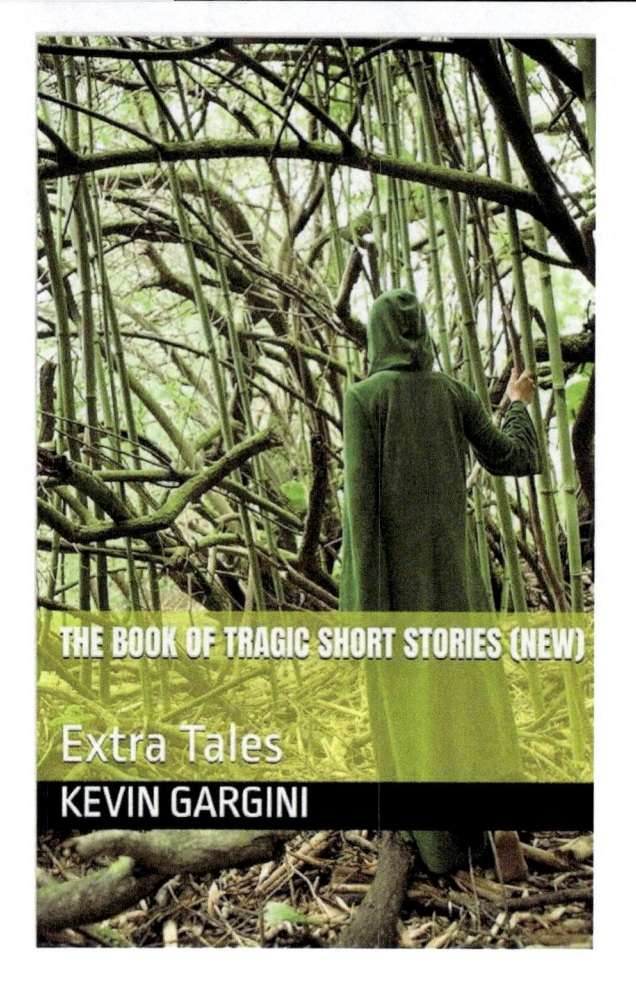

Extra Tales

KEVIN GARGINI

THE BOOK OF TRAGIC SHORT STORIES

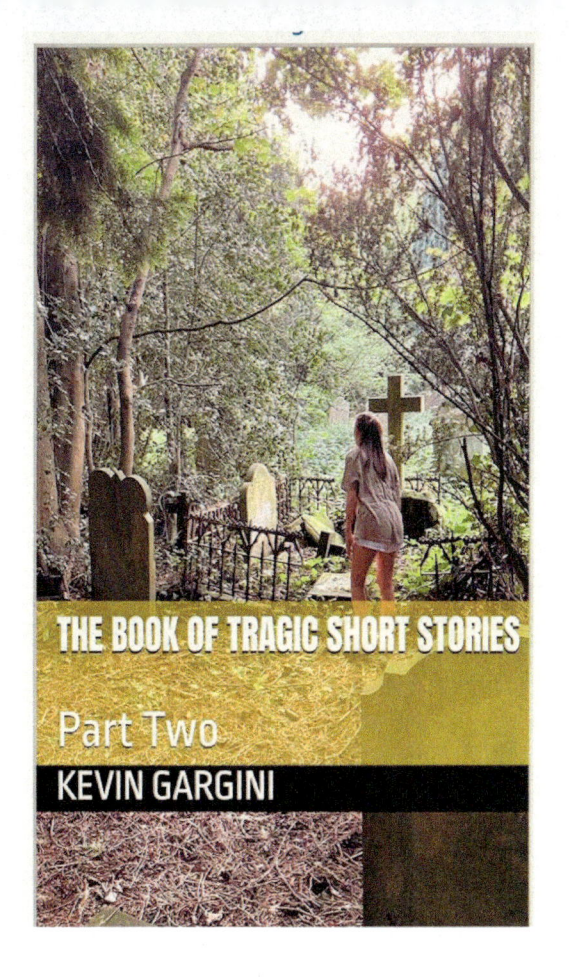

Part Two

KEVIN GARGINI

Printed in Great Britain
by Amazon